T0158939

A SERIAL SHORT

One WESTERN Town Part 3

David Quell

WESTBOW
PRESS®
A DIVISION OF THOMAS NELSON
& ZONDERVAN

Scripture quotes are taken from the King James Version of the Bible.

WestBow Press books may be ordered through booksellers or by contacting:

WestBow Press
A Division of Thomas Nelson & Zondervan
1663 Liberty Drive
Bloomington, IN 47403
www.westbowpress.com
1 (866) 928-1240

ISBN: 978-1-5127-7373-6 (sc)
ISBN: 978-1-5127-7374-3 (hc)
ISBN: 978-1-5127-7372-9 (e)

Library of Congress Control Number: 2017901353

Print information available on the last page.

WestBow Press rev. date: 03/14/2017

To my Lord and Savior Jesus Christ and to
my beloved girls Genevieve and Jilliene

1

'Blessed is the man that feareth the Lord, that delighteth greatly in his Commandments. His seed shall be mighty upon the earth, and the generation of the upright shall be blessed. Wealth and riches shall be in his house, and his righteousness endureth forever. Unto the upright there ariseth light in the darkness.' (Psm 112)

Train. Train. Train, train. Train, train, train! The train, with agitated revolving drums, drove down the metal track with a repetitious click-clack,click-clack,click-clack. The sharp sound echoed, keeping time. Winding rails abrade each incline, rolling about the elevations in a semi-circular fashion. The steam powered pistons churned, propelling the transport with haste. It was as if it were a sarcophagus that was past due for burial. The crystalline sound of the wheel on the line screamed a death knell. The mechanized movement cut through the countryside like the peeling of an apple. The friction did little to slow the train's progress. As the melded columns careened over the steel bars, it appeared to be more like a charging rhino than an iron horse. Pushing forward, the cow catcher jutted out, extricating any obstruction in its path. The blackened hull of the engine seemed to absorb all the rays of light surrounding the track. The front stack was tall and monumental, almost with an air of pride. As the locomotive chewed onward, it masticated the coal, spewing out thick bellowing cumulus puffs, one after another. The black smoke choked the atmosphere, leaving ash strewn across the landscape.

The freight cars were attached to this streamer by Herculean joints. The boxes were squared, colorful, and distinct. The painted wood created a kaleidoscope image as they moved across the background of green, brown, and grey scenery. In the viewing, all the senses became engaged. The wisps of air created by this vehicles visible vapor burned the nares. Buried deep beneath the snuffling scent, each hair stung. Below the nostrils, a swelling of saliva attempted to flood the flavor created in the clash of smoke and mucous membrane. The bold and bitter extract overflowed. Passing the tongue, the fluid was swallowed hard by a gasping gullet. Perceiving the stimuli of revolving wheels rattling on the rails, the malleus, incus, and stapes rang. The wave perceived by the auditory drum was like an arrow. Passing the bones, it collided with the cochlea, causing a crescendo of sensation. The pulsating surface forced nerve fibers to fire, conveying motion. The vibrations shook the ground. Through the quake, a visible grace could be seen. It was a sight to behold, this train.

On this day, as the serpentine shuttle slithered across the lines, more than one set of eyes were at attention. The sun was high and heavy. The heat rose from the ground in waves. The light shone bright. The radiant illumination bathed the train, as the colors moved from left to right with a pleasing reverberation. Sunlight flickered on and off the passing cars. The strobe effect dazzled, as the trees flew by. The rays and hues accented the train's movement. There were several watchers regarding that day. Looking down from the hillside vantage point were the train robbers. The band waited. They waited with evil in their hearts. They waited for the train. The train came about the curve, then drove straight away. A single command lit the fuse. The horses broke with a violent burst. Down the incline they went in a rush of muscular motion. The hooves of the rampaging horses pounded the powder underneath, thrusting up a wave of dust. The former created cloud blew in toward the train, carrying a throng of thieves. The cowboys made on a diagonal path. The oblique equine undulation swelled. It's turbulence pushed the riders parallel to the train. With rapidity, the pack ran right up to the metal wheels revolving along the rail.

The lead rider saw a boxcar with the door slightly ajar. The freighters carried a variety of products. They carried the human kind, the animal kind, and the mineral. This train transported the most precious of minerals, gold. The riders made for the entry point. The prime horse surged, stretching out with each stride. The lead steadied himself. Up and off his saddle he leapt. His hands held hard to the iron rungs running up the side of the car. The cowboy quickly employed his muscular manual momentum as he threw open the door. He stepped into the waiting dark. In turn, each of the other cowboys followed in succession.

The open entranceway allotted for the only light. The runnel of the midday sun streamed onto the floor. Glancing around, the car was filled with bales of stacked straw. The irregular rectangles were piled in perpendiculars. The straw seemed to be a bit of an oddity for this conveyance, yet an even greater peculiarity was the person seen asleep on the ground. A lone hobo lay slumbering. His only cover was a dirty hat. His face, being hidden, accentuated his unkempt attire. The hobo's shirt had few buttons. Easily noticed were the numerous areas of stress to the integrity of the cloth. The obvious overuse of the once white fabric, combined with a layer of soil, made it appear tan. The shirt was pulled out from his pants. It draped over the hobo's belt. The frayed ends pointed to the tattered trousers on which every inch seemed to be wrinkled or torn.

The cowboys looked at each other as smiles of mischief formed across their faces. The lead strode over to the snoring lump of humanity. His shadow blocked the sunlight. As the cowboy cast a cover of darkness over the reclining stowaway, he spoke.

"Get up you worthless filth." The cowboy gave the hobo a more than gentle tap with his boot. From behind the grime, the hobo retorted.

"What?" The cowboy was visibly enraged. His patience thin, he shouted.

"I want you gone! Get up, we have business to conduct."

The hobo lay motionless. After a time, he replied. "'And the servant of the Lord must not strive, but be gentle unto all men, apt to teach, patient. In meekness, instructing those that oppose themselves. If God peradventure will give them repentance to the acknowledging of the truth. And that they may recover themselves out of the snare of the devil, who are taken captive by him at his will.'" (2 Tim 2:24) The cowboys, bewildered,

4

stood transfixed for a second. The perplexed poachers attempted to process the learned language that had just flowed from the vagrant. In their hesitation the hobo again spoke. "Or, maybe I am not that patient a servant."

As the hobo's words struck the cowboys ears, a new resounding pitch hit. The impact of a growl grew from a low octave tone. Suddenly, a shadow sprang from the dark, engaging the cowboys. There was wailing and gnashing of teeth. One cowboy crashed against the box car wall. An enormous weight had come down upon him out of the blackness. He was rendered unconscious, struck by a charging carnivore. Two cowboys reached for their weapons. Each was met by a sharp spike. One impaled a cowboy's thigh. The other struck the second's shoulder. The cowboys reached for their wounds in pain. In fear, one cowboy turned to run. He jumped from the moving car, disappearing into the passing daylight. The last cowboy stood near the open exit. He quickly pulled himself over the top of the door's frame. His footsteps were heard racing across the roof, as he made his escape from atop the moving train.

In the middle of the murky confusion, a hand firmly grasped the arm of the cowboy with the lacerated shoulder. It was a strong grip, unyielding. The sensation was followed by a powerful perception of iron being wrapped around the cowboy's wrists. The cowboy was now shackled. He attempted to pull away from the confinement but the force of his motion was cut short by a tight metal chain fixed to the boxcar's wall. The cowboy pulled and pulled with all this might, to no avail. He looked over towards the resting place of the hobo. The space was no longer occupied. A muscular form now became apparent standing next to the cowboy as he realized he had been duped.

While standing strong, the hobo was met from behind with a mighty blow. It was followed by an encapsulating arm around his neck. Air refused to be inspired. The hobo struggled to release himself from the sinewy fetters. No such deliverance came. The hobo struck back by firmly landing an elbow into the cowboy's upper abdomen. It buried deep into his gut. The energy of the strike propelled the cowboy in the reverse. His grip however did not loosen. Struggling with much difficulty to overcome his restraint, the hobo reached down clasping the knife handle protruding from the cowboy's thigh. Turning it slightly, the cowboy screamed. His grasp released. The cowboy dropped to one knee. Before he could cradle the agony in his hands, they were met by a clash of copper cuffs. He, like his partner, was fastened by links to the boxcar.

The hobo glanced over at the third cowboy. He saw the outline of the large gray wolf standing above. His teeth were drawn. His nostrils flared as he growled. The cowboy was unmoving. The hobo stepped out from the dark into the light. His face was now seen in full vision. It was Quaid, Marshall Quaid. The Marshall raised his arm, pointing out from the clattering car. "Poe protect!" He shouted. As he did a dark form of a large gray wolf sprang forth. The thylacine apparition hurled himself through the open entrance. Poe hit the ground in full stride. Running at top speed, Poe pushed forward in pursuit of the elusive escapee. Quaid smiled, then turned his attention back to the remaining cowboy. He glanced up in an attempt to locate him. Quaid leaned out from the car's confines.

In an effort to gauge the cowboy's whereabouts, he turned his head on a slight angle. Quaid's eyes captured a flickering light moving towards the engine. Quaid felt his heart quicken. It raced, right along with the repetitive pulsation of the train's propellant wheels. The pounding grew as the power of the air's blasts blew. Across his features, the rush of wind matched the rush of blood through his veins.Quaid's face felt numb. His eyes teared. His nose burned.nQuaid concentrated on the moment. At this point, the use of bullets and blades would be blunted by the air's energy, he thought. He would have to rely on close quarters combat. Quaid pursued on foot.

Quaid grabbed the edge of the roof with both hands, steadying himself. Performing a pull-up, he saw the cowboy fleeing. In the center of the sun's blinding light the traitor turned toward Quaid. The cowboy drew his weapon. He squeezed the trigger. Projectiles rained down on Quaid. The sound of metal striking the boxcar resounded. Quaid tucked back his head like a tortoise. Once the barrage of bullets had come to a close, Quaid took a deep breath to clear his thoughts. He slowly peered around the corner of the car to ascertain his enemy's position. No cowboy was seen atop the train. Quaid furthered his gaze. While doing so, he felt a sudden jolt. A back-and-forth motion shook him from his foothold. Quaid strengthened his grasp, stabilizing his stance.

Quaid saw the rear cars slide away. Two cars up, the cowboy had uncoupled their connection. Quaid's mind sped, searching for a solution. In a moment of desperation, Quaid reached to his back, drawing a battle axe. In one motion, he flung it at the retreating thief. End over end it flew. The axe struck the target hard. It landed, however, not in the cowboy's frame, but in the boxcar's. The cowboy laughed loudly.

"Nice try Marshall," shouted his adversary. "You are nothing like your father, and neither is your aim." Quaid groaned. A scowl of disgust at the cowboy's comments came across his face. The disapproving frown was met by an ever expanding determination. Under his breath, Quaid whispered. "Right." He lifted up his hand, holding a lasso which was firmly attached to the handle of the axe. It's presence had gone unnoticed by the cowboy in his celebration. The enemy turned his back as the cars dropped off. The speeding caravan approached a very large ravine. Quaid saw the mountainside dive down deep. A wooden matrix, like a spiderweb, held the track high above the river's rushing water. This would be his chance, he thought. Quaid pulled on the end of the knot tight. The cars hit the overpass at full steam. Quaid looked up ahead, gauging his foe's position. Quaid leaned back, tightening the wire with his weight. Now, with the train traveling over the gorge, Quaid let fly his body like a pendulum. The cowboy perceived a shadow from his periphery. The reflective image of a man moving across the towering supports had caught his eye. The cowboy again drew his weapon. He fired rapidly, emptying his revolver. His bullets passed by the swinging Quaid. Having eluded the projectiles, Quaid landed safely on the other side of the moving train. Quaid grabbed the metal appendages of the boxcar. He released the rope. Quaid had successfully maneuvered to the front of the cowboy. Having uncoupled the cars, the cowboy was cornered. Trapped, the cowboy went on the offensive. He employed another revolver from his holster. Running wildly and firing at will, the cowboy forced Quaid down in between the gap of the boxcars. Quaid drew a blade from his belt and waited for the onslaught to cease. He stood, then threw the knife. It missed it's mark. However, to avoid the cleaver, the cowboy abruptly slung to one side. Spinning, the cowboy's footing gave way to torque. He slid down hard onto his abdomen. The cowboy's weapon dropped from the train into the depths of the abyss. Sliding further to the edge the cowboy's discordant mass betrayed him. He reached for the surface but only held air. The cowboy's hips slung over the side. Quaid lept to the car's top, reaching forward with haste. Quaid attempted to clasp his enemy's hand. Falling prey to gravity, the cowboy dropped to his death. Quaid simply hung his head. Seeing the loss of life sickened his stomach.

When the slowing cars stopped, Quaid debarked from the train. Quaid crossed the tracks from the ravine to land. There he sat his hulking habitus down at the base of the tree. The shade afforded Quaid some relief from the heat. His sweat dripped from under his hat, and down his face. Quaid removed his conical covering and wiped his brow. He looked back at the overpass. Too much death, he thought. Quaid's mind became contemplative. He was saddened by the lost soul. Every sinner deserves a second chance, he thought. Quaid was reminded of his Lord's words. " 'What man of you having a hundred sheep, if he lose one of them, does not leave the ninety-nine in the wilderness, and go after that which is lost until he find it?'" (Luke 15:4)

Quaid's meditation on death ceased. His reflections turned to that of new life. The new life he had created was with his wife. Kristin Quaid was pregnant; and full-term now. Quaid smiled at the memory of her face. He recalled her countenance kindly. Kristin had a most pleasing appearance. Quaid remembered her alabaster skin. It was full and soft, almost glowing. She had deep opulent blue eyes. Each sparkled like stars. Her blonde locks were naturally curly. The length of her hair fell not far from her shoulders. Her smile was enchanting. The white bright enamels behind the supple smile turned at the corners of her lips, lighting Quaid up like a bonfire. She was simply beautiful. The Marshall's wife was built like most western women, somewhat thin. She was a pretty little lady. Her heart, however, was as vast as the whole outdoors. Greater than her formed features, was her compassion. Always warm and receptive, she had a gracious manner. Kindness was her constant companion. Kristin had a unique ability to console. She made everyone she met feel special. Quaid's mind continued on his journey. He traveled back to a more tranquil time when he and Kristin ventured out for a picnic lunch. Quaid drove the hitch through the beautiful countryside. The foliage was green against a field of blue sky. The hills seem to roll down from the clouds as an aquamarine ocean flows from sea to shore. The light was a bright yellow. It bathed the trees in a gentle shower of particles. Quaid slowly brought the wagon to a stop. Pulling back on the reins, the horses halted their forward motion. Quaid climbed off his perch. They had come to a sunny spot filled with flowers, vegetation, and tall grass. It was dreamlike. Quaid laid a patchwork blanket down on the soft earth. He reached into the back of the wagon and withdrew a large wicker basket. He placed it with care beside the blanket. Then with refinement, Quaid walked around to the opposite side of the hitch. He took Kristin's hand, helping her down from her pedestal. It was serene. Kristen knelt. She then reclined fully, taking solace in the shade. Quaid looked upon his wife. Her dress was a singular color, white. It appeared new. There were no loose threads. No frayed ends. Windswept, it blew gently with the breeze. Every curve came alive. Taking off her shoes, Kristin's toes reveled in the release of their confinement. Quaid was relaxed. He laid down in the left lateral position. His hand supported his head such that he could gaze upon his love. Love, Quaid thought. Love was the only possession worth having in life. To possess love was to know God. To know God, to love God, was to know the secret of life. Quaid's heart sang as he sat. He recalled this solitary passage .'Beloved, let us love one another. For love is of God. And everyone that loveth is born of God, and knoweth God.' (1 John 4:7) Quaid regarded his love, and smiled.

2

"Marshall!" A loud voice rang out, awakening Quaid from his daydream. He saw John Henry atop his Mustang riding in a hard line. As John Henry drew near, Quaid's cognitive solitude transformed. He felt a sinking feeling. And uneasy regurgitant rose in his throat. It burned a bit, souring the taste buds of his tongue. With full fortitude, Quaid stood up tall. Digging his feet firmly in the dust, Quaid awaited the oncoming verbal assault.

"Marshal! Marshal!" came the cry. It was more of a lamentation than a proclamation of good news. The tone was one of mourning. Quaid's heart stopped. His apprehension pulsated. Quaid's ears pricked up for what was to follow. John Henry drove his horse right up to the spot where Quaid was standing. He pulled back firmly on the reins. The mustang stopped abruptly. The dust blew over Quaid in a cloud. Through the haze, Quaid blinked. He then focused. Quaid looked directly into John Henry's eyes. Quaid tried to glean information from John Henry's expression. His face was forlorn. It added to the anxiety. The desolation, like a virus, quickly spread across to Quaid. In a shiver, his being shook ever so slightly. It was not visibly noticeable, however. The tremor tarried, then propagated down to his boots. Quaid swallowed hard. Worry turned to dread. Quaid waited for the next words for what it seemed like days.

"Marshall, it's Kristin," said John Henry. Quaid stood still, his limbs frozen. His heart pushed blood to every extremity with a pounding pulse pressure. Quaid was afraid to ask the question bursting from his mind.

"What is it?" Quaid inquired.

"The doctor said for you to come home. Come, now," responded John Henry. Despite his fear, Quaid moved quickly into action. He gave out a loud whistle, and took off on foot. In the middle of a full run, Quaid shouted at the top of his voice, "Poe, protect!" In the distance, he could see Poe striding. The beast strained with full strength his musculature directly towards home. Poe's physique disappeared from view as a wraith in white came galloping out of the blue heavens. Angel headed right for the rampaging Quaid. Without missing a step, Quaid grabbed the pommel, hoisting himself safely into the saddle. The steed increased her speed. Quaid drove her fast through the grass, then over the hill. In an instant, neither were in sight.

Quaid rode with a determined strength. He willed his ride forward, pushing towards the wooded land separating him from his wife and child. As he entered the thicket, all became dark. It was as if the clawed hand of a giant predator clasped the sun, crushing out the light. The cold air blew. It chilled the sweat on Quaid's brow. Quaid pulled down firmly on his hat, tightening it's hold upon his head. Quaid held the reins firmly as the gale wind became a torrent. He could hear the rush of the violent current push past him. Quaid continued on, with his visage stern and unchanged by the elements.

The trees began bending to the wind's bellow. The branches reached out, striking Quaid. It stung. Over and over it stung, like bees. Quaid struggled to stay atop his ride. The trees talons slapped Quaid's face, drawing blood. Quaid pulled up his kerchief to protect his skin from the thorns. Quaid's mind pictured Dantes Divine Comedy. 'Not foliage green, but of a dusky colour, Not branches smooth, but gnarled and intertangled, not apple-trees were there, but thorns with poison'. Quaid lowered his station next to Angel's neck to avoid being struck. The arduous arbors, were angered by their failed attempt to slow Quaid's progress. They swung in fury. Quaid directed Angel through the trees. They seemed to come to life in an effort to inflict pain. Quaid's mind continued on his journey through Dante's Inferno. 'It falls into the wood, and no part is chosen for it, but where fortune flings it. There it takes root like a grain of spelt'.

The sorrowful spirits of suicide trapped in the trunks extended their boughs with force. The clouds clapped. Thunderously, they delivered streams of rain. The liquid drenched Quaid's coverings, soaking him through to the skin. Angel's shoes pounded the wet ground. The pieces of mud and grass flew from her flank. She drove on through the darkness of the downpour. Each stride was steadied by her enormous power and grace. Despite the heroics of her hurried hooves, Quaid continued to be slashed and smitten. The dark bark had bite. Every strike registered a mark of reddening pain. Suddenly a large burst exploded into Quaid's side. The sound of the blunt force of lumber colliding with bone was heard. Quaid was thrown. From his damp rest, Quaid saw Angel ramble away into the night. Quaid felt lost. Stunned, he shook his head to clear the cobwebs. Abandoned and alone, Quaid needed an ally. He decided to pray. "'I will love thee, O Lord, my strength. The Lord is my rock,and my fortress, and my deliverer. My God, my strength, in whom I will trust, my buckler, and the horn of my salvation, and my high tower. I will call upon the Lord, who is worthy to be praised, so shall I be saved from my enemies.'" (Psm 18:1)

Quaid stood up. He reached down and picked up his hat. He checked the rope that adorned his hip. He replaced the hat back onto his head. An indomitable spirit swelled within him. It incited his resolve. Quaid took off on foot, racing through the remaining brush. He came to a small clearing. At it's end was a body of water. Quaid ran right up to the edge of the river's rapids. The sound of rushing water flowed into Quaid's auditory system. Quaid could see the white caps washing from the tops of the waves. He evaluated his options. There was no place to cross without suffering through the surf. Quaid had to act quickly. He thrust himself feet-first into the river. It was cold. The temperature change created an apneic episode. It gave Quaid an uneasy sensation. He recalled his training as a young boy. Uncle Blue had taught him to remain calm in rough water situations. His memory gave him confidence. Keeping his head up, Quaid's arms lashed out in a circular motion. The crests of the current's power poured over his head. The water gurgled in and out of his mouth as he swam against the waves. Quaid cut across laterally.

He swam with the flow of the fluid, avoiding the undertow. He gasped to gain much needed oxygen. Quaid continued forward. His arms went up and out of the surface, driving him closer to the river's edge. Upon approach, Quaid saw that the bank was on a much higher plane than that of the water. Swimming to the opposite side had been a challenge. Getting himself out of the drink would prove more difficult. Quaid attempted to grab at the elevated border to no avail. Each attempt simply pushed him back further into the flowing fury. Quaid began to tire. His hat was lost to the force of the watercourse, but not his nerve. The whitewater continued to agitate Quaid. He attempted to whistle for help. No sound was made. All was muffled in the crushing swell. Quaid looked up in an effort to figure a way out. In the dark he saw the outline of his equine companion coming back for him. Quaid bobbed like a bottle. Spinning, crashing, dropping, he was dragged by the energy downstream. Angel galloped in a parallel course to Quaid. With a renewed hope, he reached for his rope. From off his hip, he raised the line. Rotating it above his head, Quaid released the life preserver across the divide. The lasso landed around the horn of Angel's saddle. She retreated, tightening the cord. The powerful pull ejected Quaid from his water-filled entrapment. He rolled out supine. Quaid laid still, catching his breath. His chest rose and fell filling the alveoli with much needed air. Quaid's clothes were soaked. The weight held him backside down on the earth, like a topsy-turvy turtle. Quaid opened his eyes wide. He gathered his thoughts. Quaid so wanted to remain sedentary. After a short while, he realized the importance of continued movement. He needed to get home, and get home fast.

Quaid was startled by Angel's loud snort. It broke his concentration. He leapt up. Quaid quickly mounted his horse, riding with fierceness into the blackness. The rain slowed. The clouds parted. This sun shone through the atmosphere, revealing a rainbow. The colors lead the way home. Drawing near, Quaid pushed even harder. He could see the outline of the old wooden structure in the distance. There was a carriage out front. Quaid concluded that his wife was in labor. He pulled hard on the reins. Quaid dropped down from Angel's back and ran onto the porch. Reaching out his arm, he threw open the front door. Entering, he immediately heard a loud commotion. The clamoring came from the back. It was an amalgamation of expression. The loud voices wailed through the closed barrier of the bedroom door. One was clearly not human. The howling of Poe was heard above the other cries. Quaid's body quivered. The growl was of one engaged in defense. Something was terribly wrong. Quaid felt it down in his bones. He burst through the doorway and into the room. As Quaid entered, he saw Kristin lying on the bed. The sheets were saturated in red. There was so much red, it pooled under her pale body. And the excess dripped down onto the floor. Poe cornered the nurse and the doctor. Behind Poe, crying and damp, was a newborn girl.

Quaid shouted, "Poe! Hold!" Poe sat. Yet, he continued to keep a strong vigilance. Quaid hastened to Kristin's side. He slid slowly onto his hind legs, kneeling as if to pray. Quaid took Kristin's blood-soaked hand into his.

"My love, can you hear me?" asked Quaid.

"Yes," she said softly.

"Are you in any pain?" Quaid questioned quietly.

"I have a terrible headache," Kristin replied. "And I feel so weak."

"You have lost a lot of blood my love," said Quaid. "But I can still feel your pulse in my hand." Quaid paused as he looked deep into her eyes of blue. "Do not trouble yourself, just now. You will recover," he said as the moisture gathered, then rolled over his cheek.

"No my love, I will not," she said in whisper. Quaid swallowed hard. Shocked by his beloved's pronouncement his eyes widened. Kristin's voice weakened, yet she continued. "Promise me Jacob… Promise me, that you will never leave…" The words trailed off as her respirations slowed. Quaid waited. Nothing further came.

Quaid replied with conviction. " I will not leave you my love, ever," he said affectionately.

Kristin looked longingly at Quaid. She whispered, "Jacob, never leave my baby." Then, she simply slipped from activity to stillness.

Quaid sat back. His head hung as the despair gave way to grief. He let her lifeless hand drop. Quaid covered his face refusing to believe. After a time, he rose. He stumbled to the door. At the entryway, Quaid stopped. He leaned on the frame with his shoulders for support. He remained still, his back facing the bed. The nurse and doctor looked over at the Marshall for some kind of guidance. No sign came. There was no movement, no speech, only silence. A baby's cry broke the dead air. Quaid turned his head in the direction of the child. In silhouette, there was a release of a tear from Quaid's green eyes. It ran down his cheek leaving a trail of saline. Quaid could look no longer. He turned and ran. Quaid's sorrow exploded into anger as he sped from the house. He accelerated. Quaid increased his velocity as the burning pain expanded. His heart felt like a ball of fire that was about to violently flash from his chest. His inspirations quickened. He blew out the air as if to rid himself of an inner evil. Finally, in frustration, Quaid screamed. He ran. He ran and he ran, until he could run no more. Exhausted, Quaid collapsed atop his knees. His lungs pulled in oxygen like a dying man. Quaid wept loudly. His face, red and swollen, continued to produce tears. Unaware to Quaid, a black pair of boots stood watching. From that vantage point came a susurrous request.

"Please, let me go to him," said the voice in the distance.

"Help is coming," came an answer out of the ether.

As the response rode out over the wind, a furry friend made himself known to Quaid. Poe came to his master's aid. He rubbed firmly against Quaid's side. The wolf had let him know that he was not alone. Quaid put his arms around his partner. He held him crying . "My friend," said Quaid. "My Love is no more." His heart broke. It was too much to bear.

The day was damp. It rained. The drops fell like a child's sorrow. They filled the earth, as if all the angels in heaven had lamented without cessation. The sun hid behind the haze. Sadness hung in the clouds, thickening the mist. The trees bent down in the dusty gloom. The birds of the air did not fly. On the hill stood six figures. They consisted of one man and one woman, a large gentleman of color holding a small child's hand, a priest, and Jacob Quaid. The doctor, his nurse, John Henry and Samantha, were all that attended. The large black umbrellas kept the elements off of the participants; all except

Quaid. He stood with no coverings. Cold and wet, Quaid felt nothing. He was numb. Quaid stared down into the grave. Deep in the hole, he saw the droplets deflecting off the casket. Quaid's consciousness was blunted. He could shed no more tears. Quaid turned inward to his anger.

The priest spoke with an open Bible. The doctor held out his umbrella to protect the pages from the rain. Quaid never looked up. He was transfixed. There was no interruption of his gaze through with the deluge. The priest concluded the ceremony with Isaiah.

"'He will swallow up death in victory, and the Lord God will wipe away the tears from off all faces.'" (Is 25:8)

Quaid's ears heard the words. Still no comfort came. His heart remained heavy. The priest closed his Bible. He made the sign of the cross over the burial plot, then moved off. The doctor and his nurse followed. John Henry glanced over at Quaid. He could not see his friend's face, only his grief. John Henry wanted to console his brother. He walked over to Quaid. As he drew near, John Henry held Samantha's hand tighter. Standing in front of his friend, he searched for the right words. "Jacob, we are truly sorry your loss," he said. Quaid remained still, not speaking. John Henry continued," You know that we loved her." There was no response. Quaid was mute. John Henry hesitated. He bowed his head in frustration. With no hope of solace, John Henry turned away. The sullen Quaid was statuesque. Unmoving in the rain, Quaid continued to drown in his sorrow. He saw the casket but could not believe the circumstance. Someone had to fill in the dirt, he thought. The mound was now muddied by the rain. Quaid walked over to the elevation, and took up a shovel.

He started spreading the brown sandy covering over the coffin. His muscles strained with each stroke. Quaid welcomed the pain. He wanted to feel. He wanted to feel anything, except heartache. Quaid concealed the emptiness of loss. Quaid worked harder and faster. His mind's memory took him back to the day before. The thought cut through his consciousness. Quaid toiled with a driven diligence. He completed the task without interruption. Once done, Quaid turned to see the headstone. The vision made it all to real. Covered in mud, Quaid dropped to his knees. Released from the hold of his resentment, more tears fell.

Long hours became long days. The long days led to more long hours. Quaid's sadness turned him to drink. Habitual melancholy drove him to compulsion. He began to swallow his despair daily. The alcohol altered his actuality. Fleeing from reality was no escape. Quaid became a prisoner. He drank to end the pain. Some days, he just drank for no apparent reason. He drank to end his life. Months of pouring death down his throat started to affect Quaid's work. Less and less, would Quaid dress and ride into town. The jailhouse was quiet for days at a time. Knowing Quaid required help with a newborn, the nurse came to the ranch day after day to deliver care. Often Quaid came to the door but later could not be found. Quaid's clothes became unkempt. He neither shaved nor bathed. His weight fell, and his eyes drew dark. Quaid's despondent nature was noticed by the nurse. His physical and mental changes caused her to voice her concerns to John Henry. John Henry could no longer stay silent. He rode directly to Quaid's residence. John Henry rapped loudly on the door. After a time, Quaid appeared. He was disheveled and drunk.

"Marshall are you coming to town soon? " inquired John Henry.

"Deputy, you can handle things for now," replied Quaid.

"How long will 'for now' be, Marshall?" asked John Henry. "It has been weeks already. I am concerned."

"Do not trouble yourself with me, Deputy," said Quaid.

"My name is John," he replied. "And I am your friend, remember?" Quaid looked away. He searched for words that he could not find.

"I am fine, John," replied Quaid after a time.

"If you are fine, then come to town with me today," John Henry challenged.

"I am sorry John, but I have a young mouth to feed," said Quaid.

"Then pack up her things and come to visit Sam and me," he said.

"I cannot," said Quaid. "I am sorry, I just cannot." Quaid closed the door leaving his friend standing silent in his apprehension.

One year passed. That year became two. In despair, Quaid found himself on his knees. He recited his father's favorite prayer, Psalm 23. "'The Lord is my shepherd, I shall not want. He maketh me to lie down in green pastures; he leadeth me beside the still waters. He restoreth my soul. He leadeth me in the paths of righteousness for his name's sake. Yeah, though I walk through the valley of the shadow of death, I will fear no evil; for thou art with me. Thy rod and thy staff they comfort me. Thou preparest a table before me in the presence of mine enemies. Thou anointest my head with oil, my cup... my cup... my cup...'" (Psm 23) Quaid could not continue. Grief filled his heart as the teardrops filled his eyes. Quaid could not contain himself. He cried loudly. His shoulders shook as his body heaved up-and-down. In a full display emotion, all hope poured out of his soul. Quaid wanted it to end. In desolation, he implored his God. "Father I am not worthy to receive you, but only say a word, and I will be healed." Silence. No sign would come thought Quaid. After a pause, he heard a voice from across the void. "Daddy?" came the muffled sound. He held fast. Quaid was unsure exactly what his ears had just perceived. Out of the dark, again it came. "Daddy?" The barely audible speak struck Quaid like a millstone. Stunned, Quaid turned to locate the sound. There cowering in the corner of the room was Josephine. Quaid's daughter had her eyes fixed upon her father. Seeing her, Quaid struggled to stand.

"Daddy, are you well?" Josephine asked.

Quaid steadied himself. He looked towards the heavens and closed his eyes. Quaid's emotion flowed. He attempted to wipe his face dry. Responding, Quaid's sentence structure broke apart.

"No...No, my Beloved... I am not well." replied Quaid. He halted his speech, holding his respirations. "But you have made me better." Quaid moved quickly to his little girl. He bent down and enclosed her in his massive frame. Josephine let herself go limp as her father held her tight. "I love you, Joey," said Quaid.

"I love you too, Daddy," said Josephine. Quaid let go his grip. He placed his hands on her demure shoulders.

"Oh my Beloved, I am so sorry," said Quaid.

"For what?" asked Josephine.

"For not accepting my gift from God," replied Quaid. Josephine looked longingly at her father, not quite comprehending. Quaid continued. "You… You are my most beloved gift." Josephine smiled.

"I am glad you are feeling better, Daddy," she said.

"So am I," said Quaid. "So am I."

3

Quaid grew strong. It was a happy strong. Love gives one an indomitable strength. His love for his gift made him that way. Quaid spent all his hours with Josephine. He grew as she grew. Their love grew together. Quaid taught his daughter the correct manner of speech, the virtue of etiquette, and most important the significance of spirituality. Quaid enjoyed his time with his Josephine. She was a very curious child. She longed for knowledge. Quaid knew that he could not keep her confined forever. She deserved an education. She needed social interaction. Josephine would go to school. Quaid had to learn to let go.

Quaid accompanied his little girl to the schoolhouse each morning. Every afternoon, he would escort her home. Quaid looked forward to the long walks. As they strode from home to town and back again, Quaid conversed with his young lady. In the guise of daily small talk, Quaid connected to his most precious gift. As they travelled, Quaid spoke of philosophy, music, and literature. He filled the majority of the time discussing his favorite subject, God. His heart was full. Quaid's parenting was stringent but he only had one firm rule; never leave without saying, 'I love you'.

One fine spring morning, Quaid found himself behind his time. Josephine, as usual, was not running late. "Are you coming, Daddy?" asked Josephine.

"Yes. Please wait, I will be right there!" he shouted.

"I have to get started," Josephine said as she walked out the door. Quaid rushed, not yet finished dressing. He ran to the door in an attempt to catch his little girl.

"What about our one rule?" Quaid exclaimed into the growing light of the sunrise.

Josephine walked with purpose. The day outside was blissful and bright. She turned onto the familiar path leading into town. Through the wooded landscape she went happily. Josephine took in all the sights and sounds nature had to offer. The trees were tall. The leaves were green and glowing. The birds sang. She saw butterflies flutter in and out of the brush. Further down the trail, a small brook ran through the property. There, Josephine heard the bubbling of flowing water. It was so beautiful. She thought of Ecclesiastes. 'He hath made everything beautiful in his time. Also He hath set the world in their heart'. (Ecc 3:11)

Back at the house, Quaid scrambled to ready himself. He donned this hat, belt, and gun. His food lay half eaten on his plate at the kitchen table. He grabbed a hunk of bread, pushing it directly into his mouth. Quaid had left the front door ajar. Pushing it fully open, he stepped onto the porch. Looking around he saw no sign of his little girl. Again, Quaid called out at the top of his lungs. No answer came. Quaid raised his voice again. No reply. She was gone. Quaid felt cold. Panic chilled his thoughts. Reflexively, he turned to the interior of his home.

"Poe protect!" Quaid shouted. Out of the shadows sprang the beast. He ran with fury, a wild fury. Unbound, Poe raced into the wilderness. Quaid made quickly for the barn. Angel waited there. He would need her speed. Josephine continued down the path. She carried her books over her shoulder with a single leather strap. The sun felt warm. It's light radiated off the moisture of the foliage. It appeared as a thousand rainbows, one from each leaf. Josephine made her way merrily. The route rounded a corner close to the edge of the creek. As she turned, Josephine saw a small boy crouched by the muddy bank. He had his back turned to her approach. Hearing her strides, he stood, and smiled. The boy did not address her at first. Josephine stopped. Being friendly, she said, "Hello".

"Hello," he replied as a grin came over his face.

"Do I know you?" asked Josephine.

"'I know my sheep, and am known of mine,'" (John 10:14) he said.

Though slightly confused, Josephine continued to speak. "I am Josephine. What is your name?"

"I am Isa," said the boy. The boy's look was somewhat nondescript. His hair was dark with small curls throughout. He had tanned skin. His eyes were a yellow- brown. His only outstanding feature was a prominent nose. It was a proud nose. It was a virtuous nose. Unafraid, Josephine grew more curious of her new friend.

"What are you doing?" she asked. The boy stepped aside to reveal several small birds made from the mud. They were sitting in rows on the sandy slope of the creek. "Those are beautiful," said Josephine. "Did you make them?" she asked.

"All that you see," said Isa, as he smiled widely.

As the words rolled off his lips, a loud growl came out from deep in the woods. A large gray canine came bounding full stride at the boy. Poe headed right at Isa. Josephine screamed in desperation, "Poe, no!" The wolf continued on his path unabated. Isa raised his right hand. "Peace, be still!" he said. The rabid wolf abruptly stopped. Josephine stood stunned, but relieved. She then inquired of her friend. "Isa are you hurt?" she asked.

"No," he responded. The boy walked over and addressed her directly. "I have found favor in you," he said.

"You seem nice too," replied Josephine.

"Maybe you could play with me?" asked Isa.

Josephine felt disappointment as she responded to the boy's query. "I am sorry, Isa, but I cannot. I am late for school already," she said.

The boy was visibly upset. He turned away from Josephine's gaze. He took several steps forward then stopped. Isa clapped his hands together forcibly. A sound like thunder cracked. It was followed buy an even more powerful uproar, the flapping of wings. The combined shrieks of avian flight exploded in waves. A massive departure arose from the ground. Josephine was startled. She threw up one arm in an effort to shield her face. Through the commotion, Josephine saw numerous birds fly out from under the feet of the boy. They quickly disappeared, soaring right into the driving sun. Still shielding her vision,

Josephine could no longer see any clay figures in the mud. Scared, she ran. She ran without stopping, through the woods. With much labored breathing, Josephine emerged at the edge of town. Her respirations slowed as she saw large columns of flame fanning out from the top of the schoolhouse. It was on fire.

Quaid sent his emissary forth. Still, he remained uneasy about Josephine's departure. His heart raced as he mounted Angel. She broke into a gallop. The pair bounded from the barn. Dashing through the woods, Angel cut, leapt, and sped full forward. Her muscles strained under the guidance of a concerned father. It took merely minutes to reach the town. Quaid's pulse pounded as the burning schoolhouse came into the view. The blowing wind incited the inferno. Quaid drove Angel closer to the structure as anxiety fueled his tachycardia.

Quaid dismounted. The conflagration consumed the surrounding oxygen, leaving him breathless. He heard the screams crying out from around the yard. Dust swirled around him. Thick black smoke bellowed into the sky. Quaid fell to his knees as time travelled backwards. He was a young boy once again, confronting the barn fire. It was like being kicked in the gut. He cringed from the muscular cramping of his stomach. He froze. The blaze brought back the memory of Quaid's worst fear. He could clearly see the loss of his father in the flames. Quaid fell further forward onto all fours. His head hung. His hands barely held his weight. Nausea overcame him. His thoughts became clouded. In his confused state, Quaid pictured his father's body burning. An emotional death burst across his consciousness. Quaid's eyes filled with moisture. Through his swollen oculars, Quaid saw a small pair of dirty sandals standing next to him.

Quaid could not contain his tears. He whispered. "'Depart from me, for I am a sinful man.'" (Luke 5:8) He then closed his eyes tight. Upon opening, there stood a small boy. He smiled gently at Quaid.

"Marshall, where is Josephine?" he asked.

With those words, Quaid's mind cleared. He had to act, and act now. His determination hardened. Quaid jumped to his feet. He ran to the horse's tie-up, and threw himself into the watering trough. Quaid became totally immersed. Once submerged, he arose from the liquid renewed, as in a baptism. Quaid pushed hard against the front door. He could feel the heat from the inside. Turning the knob, Quaid found it hot to the touch. Only his soaked skin kept the epidermis from blistering. Quaid released his grip immediately. No admittance granted. He stepped back and whistled. Angel cantered right up to his position. Since he could not easily enter, Quaid decided to employ his battle axe. Pulling it from his saddle, he strode up to the melded door with purpose. "Father open this gate, and let me in!" Quaid screamed. He swung the blade with all his might. The broadaxe burst through the wood with a loud crack. Again and again his fury drew down on the door. Quaid kicked open the remaining splinters. With no fear, he ran into the schoolhouse as the flames engulfed his form. The worried onlookers gasped. Going in, Quaid kept low. "Hello!" he shouted. "I am here to help!" Moving forward, Quaid remained below the smothering smoke. His eyes burned as he looked for the lost. Apprehension heightened as Quaid wondered what he would find. Up ahead, he heard a faded whisper. It sounded a bit like the coo of a dove. Quaid blinked to clear his vision. Lying on the floor was little

Jamie. She was on her side struggling to draw in air like a fish out of water. Quaid moved quickly to her. She was alive but weakened buy hypoxia. "Come with me my darling," said Quaid softly. "Do not be afraid." Quaid lifted Jamie up, cradling her in his arms. His eyes scanned the floor. Twelve feet away he saw a small boy. It was John. He was huddled under his desk, frozen in fear. Quaid felt the extreme energy eating away at his flesh. The flames reached high blocking his path. They held him at bay. Quaid again took to his axe. He hurled it through the fire, leaving a lasso lifeline attached to the handle ."Grab the rope, Johnny!" yelled Quaid. He reeled in the boy like a fish on a hook. Quaid pulled him out of peril, as the crackling of crumbling walls blew out around them.

"John can you walk?" asked Quaid.

"Yes," replied the boy.

"Take hold of my belt!" said Quaid. Johnny held firm and took a deep breath. Together they headed for the door. There were no other signs of life. The heat intensified. The wooden structure was giving way. Pieces of the roof rained down like brimstone. There was no more time to search. Quaid made for the exit with the two in tow. He burst out the entryway in full stride. Once outside, they hit the ground hard. Reaching safety, Quaid turned his head to see the integrity of the schoolhouse come crashing down in a heap. A smoldering framework was all that remained. Ashes rose from the rubble. Looking around, no one appeared injured. The town's people came running. They covered the children with blankets, comfort, and love. Quaid was exhausted. He rolled over supine. He saw the building reduced to glowing embers. Quaid caught the attention of the schoolteacher tending to the children. She glanced in his direction. "Where is Josephine?" she asked. Quaid's heart stopped. He leapt up and ran to the edge of the burning remains. He saw nothing. He dropped to his knees in despair. Tears filled his eyes. Not wanting anyone to see his grief, Quaid covered his face. He wept. In his lamentation, Quaid made out many muffled voices. A mental silence ensued. He blocked them out. Through the muted deafness came a high pitched utterance. It was almost angelic. "Daddy?" Quaid raised his head. His eyes focused. He wondered if his hearing had betrayed him. Again he heard, "Daddy?" And there, like a phoenix, stood Josephine.

"Daddy, I am sorry but I was late for school today," she said. Quaid hugged his little girl with all his might. Joy flowed and fell from his face. "Why are you crying?" Josephine asked. "Are you hurt?"

"No my Beloved," he said. "I feel no pain." Quaid let her go gently. He smiled widely at his little one. He gathered his emotion and said, "Let us go home. We have much to be thankful for today." The pair were not far from home. However, the walk seemed longer than usual. Quaid did not mind the extra time it took to travel. He was content. He held his Beloved's hand the whole way. Quaid decided to engage his little girl with talk of heaven. This would contrast the frightening devastation of the day. "Heaven is vast," said Quaid while walking. "'In my Father's house are many rooms. If it were not so I would not have told you. I go to prepare a place for you.' (John 14:2) That is what the Bible tells us of Heaven," said Quaid.

"Is it beautiful?" asked Josephine.

"Yes, as is our God," replied Quaid. "The Bible says, 'And he that sat was to look upon like a jasper and a sardine stone. And there was a rainbow about the throne, In sight like unto an emerald.'" (Rev 4:3)

"That does sound wonderful, Daddy. But what are the stones?" Josephine asked.

"A jasper is a clear white stone. A sardine stone is the color of blood. I believe that jasper represents the purity and power of our Lord. The sardine stone represents our Lord's shedding of blood for us," said Quaid

"You mean when Jesus died on the cross?" inquired Josephine.

"Yes, and more," said Quaid. "These stones were found on what is called the breastplate of judgment. It was a formal dressing which God instructed Moses to construct for his brother Aaron in which to wear in the temple. But on the breastplate, the sardine stone was the first stone and the jasper was the last. I believe that this retells of what our Lord once said. 'So the last shall be first, and the first last.'" (Matt 20:16)

"What does that mean?" asked Josephine.

"Our Lord was telling us that despite what little you have here on earth, if your heart is with God, you will be seen as being first in heaven. You see my Beloved, God's love is given freely; but we must also accept it freely," said Quaid.

"Yes," said Josephine. "I see. It is because He loves me and I love Him. And because I love Him, He loves me."

"Yes, exactly!" said a jubilant Quaid. "The words of a child..." he whispered under his breath.

Quaid continued his stroll while regaling. Despite his good mood, the earlier events kept breaking into his thoughts. The entire happening was a bit unsettling. How was he to protect his most precious gift. He could not be with her every minute of every day. Quaid would have to put his faith in God. He would pray for his Beloved's security. Beyond this, Quaid would employ the aid of his friends, he thought. John Henry, Samantha and even Poe could lend a hand. In thinking, Quaid's curiosity ignited. He questioned Poe's whereabouts. "Joey, have you seen Poe?" asked Quaid.

"Yes Daddy, " she said. "I saw him down by the stream."

"What was he doing?" asked Quaid.

"Following his commandment," she replied.

Quaid tilted his head slightly, not fully comprehending his daughter's statement. "We must go where you saw him last," said Quaid.

"Okay, I will show you the way," said Josephine.

Quaid and Josephine altered their course. They headed down towards the bank of the creek. They brushed by many a branch and bush without any hindrance. The wood's beauty was not lost on them, however. As they made their way, the two took in all the pleasures of the senses. The color of the greens were of the brightest green. They glittered in the gleaming light. The strong, stalwart trunks of the trees stood out like monuments. Their bark was brown and deeply crevassed from years of fissured growth. The ground appeared hard and grey yet the clay felt soft underfoot. Sound of the birds carried through the air. Bugs and bees buzzed in the branches of the underbrush. The smell of the clean crisp atmosphere adorned by fresh foliage only enhanced the experience. Father and daughter tasted the tranquility, as they went. Upon reaching the stream, Quaid saw multiple footprints in the mud. "Someone was here," he said knowingly. Quaid withdrew his side-arm. "Stay back," he said, motioning to Josephine sternly. He proceeded to follow the trail. Quaid was an excellent tracker, as was his father. He slowly strode forward. An incline with a brier lay ahead. He got low. Looking over the rise of the slope, he saw a large bear. It was dead and lying in a pool of red. The large mammal had been skinned and the carcass was left to rot. Quaid approached, then crouched to read the prints left in the silt. "Trappers," said Quaid under his breath. He peered down the trail. He could see more than just human marks, but the impressions of a canine as well. Quaid followed them quickly. They lead to a small thicket. The leaves were wide and concealing. Quaid pulled back the hammer on his pistol. No motion was seen. Quaid called out, "Poe!" A whimper became audible at the heart of the vegetation. Quaid pulled back the stems to see Poe motionless on the ground. He was gunshot. He was dying. Quaid bent down to touch his old friend. "I am sorry I was not here for you," he said. Poe's eyes turned toward his master. Quaid moved his face in close. He could hear the agonal respiration. With a lick, Poe gently kissed Quaid's cheek. He then drew his last breath. As Quaid turned away from his friend's death, he saw Josephine standing behind him.

"Is it Poe?" she asked.

"Yes," said Quaid.

"Is he…" she asked.

"Yes," said Quaid. Quaid stood, then walked away. He paused after several feet, recalling his friend fondly in his thoughts.

"Daddy!" Josephine cried. Quaid came back swiftly. He saw Josephine pointing to a patch of brown fur moving underneath the deceased. "Daddy, look! It is a baby bear!" she exclaimed. Quaid lifted up the grey wolf's body. There, completely unharmed lie a tiny cub. Josephine held him in her arms. A big smile came across her face. Her eyes lit up as she felt his warmth. "Can I keep him?" she asked. Quaid pondered a bit. The cub's mother had been slain. He had no means of support. Yet, this youth was to be a large and most ferocious beast. Quaid contemplated this concern. "Please Daddy, he needs our help," implored Josephine. She held the cub lovingly like a stuffed toy. Quaid simply smiled.

"Okay, my Beloved," he replied. "We will take him home. He likely needs nourishment." Quaid could not leave Poe in this state. He walked over to Angel. Quaid removed the axe from his pack. "Josephine take your new friend down to the creek and give him some water. I need to care for Poe." he said. Quaid continued. "Then please wait for me next to Angel until I am finished. I will be with you shortly."

Quaid dug a shallow grave in the dirt next to a tall shade tree. He placed Poe in the depression gently. Quaid covered him with earth. Once done, he knelt. It was a peaceful resting place, he thought. Quaid bowed his head and prayed. "'I cried by reason of mine affliction unto the Lord and he heard me. Out of the belly of hell cried I, and Thou heardest my voice.'" (Jonah 2:2) Quaid paused. He whispered, "I want to thank you Lord for delivering to me the finest of friends. He is in your hands now. Please take care of him." Tears filled the Marshall's eyes, as his thoughts turned to Poe in their younger years. From behind, Quaid felt the consoling touch of a small hand.

"Daddy do you feel sad?" asked Josephine.

Quaid turned. He smiled at her. "No my Beloved," he said. "I feel love... I feel love."

4

Suns rose. Suns fell. Snows came, and snows went. The landscape changed. Trees grew taller. Over that same time, so did Josephine. She developed into a slender build. She was tall for a girl. Her long limbs projected out straight. Her hair was a tressy blonde. Thin, it would whisper in the wind. Her waist was small and without curves. From head to toe she was a sketch of sleek lines. Josephine wore a bright smile. The joyful expression reached far, from one cheek to the other. Her lips were full, yet never concealing her teeth of pure white. A little pug nose painted her face. Foremost, it was Josephine's green eyes that defined her beauty. Their steel-grey glow sparkled like beryllium. She was simply lovely.

Josephine's best friend, Samantha, was a cute little lady. Her exterior appeared soft, while her interior was tough. She had dark, curly hair. Dark and wavy, it was tersely cut. Samantha's big brown eyes were compelling and compassionate. Her rounded plump cheeks dimpled when she smiled. Her grin was infectious. Samantha possessed a strong persona. She had a distinctive drive. Her manner was like that of the bull, grand and powerful. Yet, she was often as cuddly as a bear cub.

Josephine's baby bear had grown into his name, Samson. He was a large brown grizzly. His fur had a seemingly silver sheen. Samson's eyes were deep and set back from his snout. Under his black nose, his mouth held sharp razor incisors. He was big, weighing over six hundred pounds. Sampson measured three and a half feet at the shoulders. At the top of his trunk was a prominent hump. When the bear stood, he cleared seven feet. Samson was formidable. He was a beast. To Josephine, he was a gentle soul, and her constant companion. From infancy on, he had been with her. He often was held in her loving arms. The omnivore, needed for little. Josephine gave him food, water, shelter, and frequently a good grooming. She taught him a fondness for life through their play. Josephine cared for him. She loved him.

It became late in the day. Quaid grew tired. He called from the front porch to Josephine, as she completed her chores in the barn. She had watered and fed the horses. Sampson was settled as well. Josephine tarried, combing and petting her friend. She spoke to him in a quiet voice. The melody of the sound seemed to soothe Samson. He was relaxed in the hands of his human mother. At peace, he fell asleep. Josephine returned to the main house. She could smell the stew her father prepared. The light grew dim as the sun found its rest at the end of the earth. Quaid lit the lamps that lay around the interior. The two sat down together at the kitchen table to dine.

"Could you say the prayer, please?" asked Quaid.

"Certainly," said Josephine. "Bless us O Lord and these your gifts which we are about to receive from thy bounty. Through Christ our Lord, Amen."

"Thank you," said Quaid. "So, tell me, what did you do today?" he asked.

"Nothing," Josephine replied.

"As in, not a thing?" Quaid inquired snidely.

"I suppose," she retorted.

"So, I suppose, tomorrow you will be doing more nothing?" asked Quaid.

"No," said Josephine slightly irritated. "I am going to see Sam."

"Very well, my Beloved," said Quaid begrudgingly. "I think you need to get out more and interact with friends." Quaid paused caught between thoughts. "But is not tomorrow Wednesday?" he asked.

"So?" Josephine smugly responded.

"Do you not remember? It is our weekly day of reading. It is our Wednesday with William," said Quaid with a sheepish grin on his face.

"I do not like your Shakespeare, Daddy," Josephine replied.

"Come now, you enjoy the stories," he said.

"No, Daddy, I do not," she said sternly.

"Well I enjoy them," said Quaid. "Besides, it is no fun without you."

"Sorry, no," she said. "I loathe Wednesdays with William."

Quaid could see he had agitated his daughter more than usual. He decided to pull back. "Okay, okay. How about we take tomorrow off from Shakespeare?" Quaid asked.

"Fine with me," Josephine said with some disgust. "I will go see Samantha, then."

Quaid decided to restart the conversation. "So Joey, was your day a good one?" he asked.

"Yes, I guess," Josephine replied softly. There was a palpable pause.

"What is it Joey?" asked Quaid.

"I want to know of grandfather." she stated.

Quaid thought for a second. "What would you like to know?" he inquired.

"I hear things about him," she said.

"What kind of things?" asked Quaid.

"Some not so good," Josephine replied.

"I see," said Quaid.

"Daddy, I thought you could tell me the real stories concerning grandfather," said Josephine. "You know, the whole truth."

"Joey, your grandfather did not talk much about his days during the war," said Quaid. "But if it is stories you want, I know a few."

"Why yes!" Josephine exclaimed.

"Every evening your grandfather would sit on the side of my bed until I fell asleep. He loved regaling me in the telling of tales. I remember there was one he told with much passion. He called it the Fable of the Red Prince. At that time, your grandfather was a younger man, much younger than I am now. His voice was strong and comforting. His baritone delivery of each word was like music. The Fable of the Red Prince began with our hero. The Red Prince was a proud and fierce warrior.

His closest friend was the Green-eyed Knight. The prince and the knight were as brothers. They shared knowledge, language, and tradition. The Red Prince was a Master archer. The Green-eyed Knight was extremely skilled with the blade. Both were accomplished equestrians. The Red Prince was well known as a great leader throughout the land. He was honorable. The Green-eyed Knight was truly a sincere soldier. He was earnest in all his actions. One day, an emissary from the West came into the realm. He had come seeking the aid of the Red Prince. The emissary told of a race of giants that were terrorizing the tribes of the West."

"Giants? Really Daddy?" questioned Josephine sarcastically.

"Yes," replied Quaid. "Once I asked your grandfather about them. He just opened the Bible to Genesis 6 and read. '"There were Giants in the earth in those days. And also after that.'" (Gen 6:4)

"What kind of giants are you talking about Daddy?" inquired Josephine.

"They were the immoral offspring of the wicked and fallen. Their appearance was hideous. Their forms were disfigured. They had long stringy red hair. Their skin was pale, like the moon. Hard knots and bulbs burst out from under their skin. No surface seemed smooth. Their eyes were dark and sunken. They possessed not only great height but great strength. These gargantuan gargoyles preyed continuously on the innocent. These beasts did not appear human but more like the descendants of evil cast back on to the earth. They were called the Sitecah." Josephine shivered at the name. Quaid continued the narrative. "The Red Prince being a protector of all that was good, volunteered to help. He and the Green-eyed Knight rode to the lands of the West. The emissary guided them on their journey. While riding the trail through the great hills, the temperature dropped. A winter's storm created fluffy snow white pillows on the path. The flakes painted the branches of the trees. It appeared as if the mountains had aged. The Red Prince and the Green Knight became covered in the frozen moisture. As they travelled the pass, there was little or no wind making the cold somewhat tolerable. The trio moved on as the bright sun shone, illuminating the spoor. At the end of day, each erected a raging fire to keep themselves from the chill of the night. The three flames glowed brightly. The flash of the yellow and red flares reflected high into the sky. The horses who had worked hard during the daylight stood close to the burning piles of wood. The combusting stacks formed a triangle of warmth. All who were tired rested." said Quaid.

"Days passed as they made their way further west. The sun seemed to scorch the earth as they went. The heat rose, baking the ambient air. The riders perspired profusely, stewing in their own sweat. The drops of moisture rolled down from under their hats, then dripped off the end of their noses. Slowly, the horses walked on. Their skin became a shiny wet. They labored over the hot sands to their destination. Upon arriving at the emissary's camp, there came a terrifying site. All the constructs of shelter had been pillaged and burned. Many men lay lifeless on the ground. The remainder of the tribe had been taken. The Red Prince and the Green-eyed Knight assessed the situation. Both were expert trackers. They picked up the giant's trail. It led them to the home of the Sitecah. Safely outside of sight, the two watched the giant's grim activities. What they saw were ungodly acts."

"What do you mean by ungodly acts?" asked Josephine.

"It is a boy's bedtime story," replied Quaid. "Your grandfather did not want to elaborate on the details."

"If I know you, Daddy, you asked anyway," said Josephine.

"Yes, well of course," said Quaid.

"What did he say?" she asked.

"It is not really dinner conversation," he replied.

"Go on Daddy, tell me what were the ungodly acts?" inquired Josephine.

"Okay... You see, the giants ate their prey," said Quaid.

"Cannibals!" exclaimed Josephine.

"It would appear so," replied Quaid.

"That is gruesome," said Josephine.

"As I said, not exactly dinner conversation," said Quaid.

"It is a good thing that it is just a story," said Josephine.

"Yes," said Quaid. "Just a story."

Quaid went back to his food while it was still warm. After dinner, the dishes were washed and dried. The discourse desiccated as well. Josephine went directly to her room. Exhausted, Quaid did the same. The bedroom was cold and dark. In the complete silence, Quaid drifted right off to sleep. There was a knock at the door. It was a gentle rapping. Quaid opened his eyes. Looking around, it was still dark. Again a tapping came. Quaid rose. He drew up his trousers. Quaid slowly, silently, made his way to the front of the house. Arriving at the egress, Quaid stopped. He listened for a sign of who might have come calling at this hour. No sound came. Quaid's thoughts rushed. Could it be urgent? Was someone in trouble? Maybe it was an early morning delivery of some sort? Quaid felt an uneasy sensation. The eerie perception penetrated through the wood. Quaid quivered. He felt like quarry. Quaid decided to open the door gradually. He would glance at the caller, then act. Quaid hardened his resolve. He grasped the door handle and pulled back on the latch. A clash of metal broke. Quaid gently drew the door back, opening a small crevasse between it and the frame.

Quaid stood astonished. His eyes peered down on a feeble old man. His hair was thin, and grey. It swept over from one side, barely covering his cranium. His skin seemed loose and lumpy. His face was furrowed with frown lines. Age spots splattered across the canvas of his features. His nose was bulbous. His ears were large, irregular, and covered with hair. The eyes of the old man were darkened. Quaid gazed down further. The old man wore a full length black coat. It covered his extremities all the way down to his boots. As Quaid regarded him, the old man smiled. His smile seemed insidious. It was not one of happiness, satisfaction, or glee. It was of guile. His teeth had the color of ink around the edges. It gave Quaid the impression that the old man was rotting from the inside out. Quaid could feel the evil emanating from him. This was not a fragile older gentleman. This thing was demonic!

Quaid threw open the door in anger. He lunged at the ogre, wrapping his hands around his throat. Quaid squeezed forcibly. The fiend screamed. The wailing transformed the incubus from innocence to iniquity. Quaid encircled his hands tighter avoiding it's sharp claws and gnashing teeth. The spirit struggled violently. Quaid increased the pressure as the demon vigorously exerted. Quaid became enraged. He twisted his grip back and forth to subdue the enemy. His blood boiled. "You came to my house!" Quaid shouted.

Bang! Bang, bang! Quaid awoke with a bang, from his bad dream. Bang! Gunfire, he thought. The Marshall rolled out of bed. His ears pricked up. Bang! Another round of bullets stirred the silence. He pulled on his pants with haste. Quaid hustled through the house with an air of madness. He found Josephine's room empty. "Joey!" he screamed. Bang! Bang! Confused, Quaid desperately tried to locate his pistol. His eyes flashed quickly from left to right. Unable to find his six-shooter, he stumbled to the kitchen grabbing a knife. Like a cyclone, Quaid blew out the back door. Standing in the tall grass of the yard was Josephine. She was holding his revolver. The young lady continued firing across the pasture in the direction of several tin targets. Samantha stood next to her, pointing.

"What are you doing?" Quaid shouted.

"I need to learn how to shoot," yelled Josephine in reply.

"Why?" asked Quaid.

"Samantha said I did," she said. Quaid glared over at Sam angrily. Self-conscious, she turned her face from his gaze. Quaid made his way over to their position.

"Josephine," Quaid started up again loudly. "Why do you think it was okay to borrow my gun without my permission?"

"I need to protect myself, Daddy," she said. Quaid smiled. He had seen this play before. His mind went briefly back to the days on his uncle's farm. The plot seemed so familiar. A twinkle formed in Quaid's eye. He understood.

"Okay, okay," said Quaid. "I can see this is important to you." Josephine grinned. "Not today though," said Quaid. Josephine's shoulders slumped. The smile dropped from her face. Quaid, seeing the change in her countenance continued. "I will take you to someone who will teach you all you need to know. He will instruct you on the proper techniques in the care and usage of firearms." Josephine's smile returned. Her eyes sparkled as her face filled with anticipation.

"When do we start?" she asked.

"Soon," said Quaid. "First we must journey a good distance east."

"I am ready now, Daddy," said Joey.

"As I said," replied Quaid. "Soon."

The very next day, Quaid mounted Angel and rode into town. Quaid was ready for a vacation. He needed a break from being a lawman. This was the perfect opportunity to spend some time with his little lady. The trip would relieve him of the pressures of the job and allow him to enjoy his gift from God. As he rode, Quaid remained deep in thought. All had been quiet around town for many months. And John Henry was ready to take on more responsibility. He was a good deputy. John Henry had proved to be inquisitive, insightful, and incorruptible. Quaid pulled up in front of his office. He tied Angel to the post on the porch. Quaid strode up the stairs and through the door of the jailhouse. He found that John Henry had already arrived.

"Good morning, John Henry," said Quaid upon entering.

"Good morning Marshall," John Henry replied.

"John Henry, we need to talk," said Quaid.

"What about?" questioned John Henry.

"The future," said Quaid. John Henry looked at Quaid perplexed. Quaid walked over to his desk, taking a seat in his chair. He looked directly into John Henry's eyes. "John Henry," said Quaid. "You are an excellent deputy. I am proud to have you as my partner, and grateful to have you as my friend." John Henry began to feel a bit uneasy.

"Then why the talk?" asked John Henry.

"I want to promote you," said Quaid. "I want to make you sheriff." Stunned, John Henry simply stared forward.

"What does that mean?" John Henry asked after a time.

"I am leaving town for a while," said Quaid.

"No, Marshall," said John Henry. "Say it is not so."

"Do not to worry, I plan on returning," said Quaid. John Henry sat down, relieved.

"Please tell me why," John Henry implored.

"I am merely taking Josephine on a small summer vacation. School is out. And honestly, I could use a few days away from my duties," said Quaid.

"I see," said John Henry. "You and Josephine are going to get to know one another better."

"Yes," said Quaid. "We will be traveling back east."

"Very good," said John Henry rising from his chair. "A father needs to invest in his family." John Henry smiled wide and nodded.

"Agreed then," said Quaid. "You will look after the store, so to speak, while I am gone?"

"Yes, of course," said John Henry. "I will keep an eye on things."

"Good," said Quaid. "Well, I guess that is that." Quaid stood up from behind his desk, rounded the corner, and headed for the door. He turned to address John Henry one last time. "Good luck, sheriff."

"Thank you," said John Henry. "Go with God, Marshall."

Once home, Quaid readied for the long journey. Josephine came in from the barn to see the main room filled with supplies. She stopped in momentary wonderment. "What are you doing, Daddy?" she asked.

"Preparing for our trip," said Quaid. "We are going to visit family."

"I thought we had no family," said Josephine.

"There is much you need to learn my Beloved, especially now that you are getting older. One of those things is that we have loved ones all over these great United States," said Quaid.

"I thought that we were all alone after mom died," said Josephine. "Are you saying that we have relatives out there?"

"Not all family is blood," said Quaid. "Take John Henry and Samantha for instance. Are they not like my brother and your sister?" Josephine nodded in agreement. "Okay then my Beloved, please go and pack up some necessities. You can roll them in your blanket or store them in your saddlebag. I have food for a few days, and water for much more. We will leave in the morning."

"I have to take care of Samson, but I will be ready, Daddy," said Josephine.

"Ready or not, we leave at dawn," replied Quaid. He smiled softly at his daughter just to let her know that all was well. Quaid finished the preparations in silence.

Later that day, Josephine made her way over to the Colonel's old place. She needed Samantha's help in caring for Samson while she was away. Being Josephine's best friend, Samantha was well known to Samson. He saw her as a sibling. As she left, the sun was found high in the sky. The blue background was filled with wisps of white clouds. It was a glorious day. Josephine decided she would walk. She made her way through the grassy land onto the rocky plane. The terrain was rough. However, it was the shortest path. Josephine plodded along. There was little sound. Even the birds of the air did not fly that day. It seemed odd to her but not uncommon. Josephine pressed down hard on the stones underfoot. Sliding at a sharp angle, she slipped to the ground. Her body struck hard. When her cognition cleared she found herself face to face with an irate rattler. Josephine froze. The snake coiled tighter, shaking its tail with virulence. Josephine reached over with her right hand to grab her revolver. The snake leapt and stung Josephine's palm. She screamed in pain as the viper withdrew. Red liquid flowed from the wound onto the ground. With her unaffected left hand she pulled out her weapon. Pulling the trigger, the projectile blasted the serpent in two. Josephine dropped the gun. She used her left hand to support the right as the agony arose into her arm. She felt faint. Her eyes filled with fluid, blurring her vision. Out of the fog, she saw a shadow. It approached quickly. As it drew near, Josephine made out the figure of a man. She started to lose consciousness. Softly, she felt the touch of a hand cradling her wounded wrist. A rush of air blew across the bite. Josephine opened her eyes to see her friend, Isa. His lips were pursed and produced a windswept current. Josephine smiled as she felt the pain being blown out of her hand. He smiled back at her lovingly. Isa helped her to her feet.

"'Be of good cheer, it is I,'" (Mark 6:50) said Isa. Puzzled, Josephine looked down. The blood had completely washed away. And the puncture marks were barely visible. In awe, she gazed over at him.

"How?" she asked.

"'My Father worketh hitherto, and I work,'" (John 5:17) he said. Josephine did not comprehend the meaning of his words. Isa wiped the tears from her face.

"How did you find me?" asked Josephine.

"The voice of thy blood cried out to me," he said. Josephine decided that he must have heard her screams. Though still a bit confused, she was happy to see her friend.

"I am pleased to see you," she said.

"As am I," said Isa. "Shall I accompany you?" he asked.

"Yes, definitely," replied Josephine. Together they walked across the remaining land side by side. They spoke incessantly along the way. It was as if time stood still in that one western town.

The following day brought an early start for Quaid. He rose, prayed, and put on the coffee. Quaid let Josephine get a few more winks while he went out to the barn. There he saddled Angel. He also harnessed Josephine's ride, Boaz. Bo was a delight of color. His hair was sorrel, a copper-red chestnut. Even next to his majestic Angel, Bo was a bold beauty. A quarter horse with pure speed, Bo was only fifteen hands high. His size, however, seemed to be just right for the petite Josephine.

Quaid led them out of the barn into the light. The morning sun shone with the promise of a new day. Quaid felt the warmth bathe his skin. It felt good on his freshly shaven cheeks. Quaid never left home without the proper trimming and dress. It was the reflection of his mother's manner. Josephine came out the front door, down the steps, and over to Boaz.

"Shall we ride?" she asked.

"Yes," said Quaid. "But first a full meal."

"Don't you want to get an early start?" Josephine asked.

"A proper start," replied Quaid. He placed his arm around her shoulder. Quaid held his little lady tight, as she tried to pull away. "Come now, let us dine," As they walked, Quaid turned to Josephine and quipped, "Please my Beloved, stop the use of the contractions."

"Yes, father," she replied hanging her head to conceal her smirk. Quaid and Josephine strode together, back into the house, eager to break the morning fast.

5

Quaid and Josephine rode out over the plain. It was still cool despite the risen sun. No clouds could be seen, only blue. This cerulean sky covered their ride like a blanket. As far as the eye could see it was pure azure. The birds of the air flew uninhibited through the ether. The pounding of the horse's hooves was all that was audible. The rhythm was steady and strong like the beat of a heart. Quaid was content. He rode through the most beautiful landscape he knew on the top of his prized pony. He rode away from the pressures of his job. And most of all; Quaid rode next to his beloved daughter. Quaid felt pride. He felt the pride of a father. As Quaid rode, he reminisced about his own father. Only if he could see him now, he thought, he would be proud of the father Quaid had become. Quaid felt the love of his father. That love he now passed on.

Quaid and Josephine rode all day without stopping. As evening approached, Quaid looked for a good place to camp. He found a well- protected piece of ground. It was surrounded on three sides by stone. The land was at a higher level. This site allowed for direct vision of approaching predators. Quaid pointed, then turned towards Josephine. "Over there," he shouted. "We can bed for the night." Josephine nodded. The two dismounted. They proceeded to gather wood for a fire. Once the branches were piled high, Quaid ignited a roaring flame. The two sat. They warmed their tired bodies. From their packs, Quaid pulled out food and drink. Quietly they ate. Darkness followed. Josephine rolled out her blanket to sleep. Quaid tried to rest but could not. So many things ran through his head. He glanced over at Josephine. She too was awake. Josephine sat up and addressed her father.

"Daddy," she said. "Tell me of your father."

"Not much to tell my Beloved," said Quaid. "He was a man, not unlike any other." Quaid paused pondering a bit. "He was a man of faith."

"Man of faith? Grandpa?" questioned Josephine with a jeer.

"He was not a perfect man," said Quaid. "But he was a forgiven one." Quaid looked directly at his daughter. "We all are."

Josephine, visibly upset, retorted. "I heard that he was a hardened killer. A murderer of women and children."

"Who said that!" Quaid exclaimed.

"I hear things," said Josephine.

"Your grandfather was a servant . What mattered to him most was love. I saw that love. And you, are the beneficiary of that love."

"I am sorry, Daddy," said Josephine. "I did not mean to offend you. I simply need to know the truth."

"You will," said Quaid. "You will, in time." Quaid looked to change the conversation. He glanced around camp, and an old story came to mind. "You know Josephine," said Quaid. "This reminds me of a tale my father once told."

"Another fable?" asked Josephine.

"Not exactly," said Quaid. "He told me that if life ever became unbearable, I should go to the desert. There, I should build three large fires. Each was to be as high as my head. Then I should light the trinity of flame, and wait."

"Wait for what?" asked Josephine.

"Charity," said Quaid.

Josephine looked at her father with curiosity. She did not know how to comprehend his response. She reflected for a moment. "Love," she said. "Maybe he meant it to mean love." Josephine paused. "I guess we could all use a little more love in our lives," she said.

Quaid felt his throat tremble. He was saddened to think that his Beloved would want for love. He would change that, he thought. "Yes," said Quaid in reluctant agreement. "Now let us get some sleep." As the words rolled over Quaid's tongue, he knew he would not rest that night.

Morning came, as it does, undaunted. Quaid rose with the sun. As he stood, he felt every muscle, bone, and joint, ache. Even his hair hurt, he thought. Quaid walked over to his sleeping beauty. He woke Josephine gently. "Time to rise and shine," said Quaid.

"What?" asked Josephine, rubbing her eyes.

"'Arise, shine, for thy light is come,'" (Is 60:1) said Quaid.

"What does that mean exactly?" asked Josephine.

"It is from Isaiah. It means to be at your best for the glory of the Lord has risen upon thee," said Quaid.

"Okay, then," replied Josephine, getting up. She knelt on one knee. Bending forward, Josephine rolled up her bedding. She tied it up neatly. Josephine stood. "Shall we ride?" she asked.

"Yes," said Quaid. "But first we will eat." Quaid walked over to his saddle, now occupying space on the ground next to a dying fire. He pulled out some bread. Along with it, he withdrew some rather smelly cheese.

"Wow!" exclaimed Josephine. "That odor is horrid!" She looked in dismay at her father. "Do you expect me to eat that?"

"Nothing like a good piece of stinky cheese," replied Quaid.

"Really?" Josephine asked sarcastically. "Just coffee. No pungent curd for me."

Quaid placed the coffee pot over the fire. He sat. He waited. Josephine waited with him, in silence. Quaid remained still and introspective. Josephine knew her father well. She left him to his thoughts. After breakfast, the two saddled their horses. They rode all day, not speaking. It was as if it was some kind of contest to see who would give in first. The day was long, dusty, and hot. Quaid tried to drink in the day, swallowing its grandeur, while nourishing his soul. They were many days into the desert. Quaid and Josephine rode on through the elements to the east. At night, Josephine stared at the stars. She dreamed. She dreamed the dreams that dreamers dream. Gazing into the heavens, Josephine reflected on God. How wondrous was His creation; she thought. And how great was His love. She prayed. "'I will love thee, O Lord, my strength. The Lord is my rock, and my fortress, and my deliverer. My God, my strength, In whom I will trust; my buckler, and the horn of my salvation, and my high tower. I will call upon the Lord, who is worthy to be praised; so shall I be saved.'" (Psm 18:1)

Quaid had remained quiet throughout the evening. Josephine decided to engage him. "Where are we going, Daddy?" she asked.

"Well Ms. Quaid, I have to see a man about a dog," said Quaid smiling.

"What does that mean?" asked Josephine.

"It is an expression," replied Quaid.

"Not a good one," retorted Josephine.

Quaid attempted to explain. "It is from a play," he said.

"More of your Shakespeare, or Poe?" Josephine queried.

"Heavens, no," said Quaid. "It is from the play, The Flying Scud."

"Sorry I asked," Josephine whispered under her breath. After that, she laid back and took to sleep.

After days of riding, the two arrived at their destination. It was a rundown farm house. The old wooden structure stood back from the dirt road. Fields of tall tan grass surrounded it on all sides. As the duo approached, Quaid slowed Angel to a walk. He reached over and grabbed the reins of Boaz. "Whoa!" said Quaid loudly. "We will walk from here."

"Why?" asked Josephine.

"You are to trust your father," said Quaid. He looked over at his daughter to see a sour stare. Quaid knew full well what that look meant. Before Josephine could say a word, Quaid addressed her. "Josephine this situation is complex. Please allow me to guide us through." Josephine gave a glance of concern.

She believed in her father. He would only speak the truth. She gave a nod of confidence.

"Yes Daddy," she replied.

"Good," said Quaid, while dismounting ."Now whatever occurs, stay completely still." Quaid extended his arm to his daughter. "Take my hand." They proceeded slowly on foot, hand in hand. As the tandem walked, they created a crushing crunch underfoot. Yards from the road, Josephine saw a malformed mailbox. The signpost stood like an ominous omen. There, Quaid stopped. "Remember our deal," said Quaid. He squeezed Josephine's hand tight. "Hold firm," he muttered. After a long pause, Quaid shouted. "Sergeant Danbeck show yourself! It is Quaid!" Bang! Out of nowhere came a gunshot. The bullet knocked Quaid's hat from his head. Quaid was not moved. He fired back with words. "Sergeant, hold your fire!"

Out of the stillness came a voice. "The colonel is dead!" Another shot rang out, ripping through Quaid's clothes at the shoulder. The round did not strike the skin. Josephine clasped her father's hand tighter.

"Be strong," murmured Quaid to Josephine. "And do not move." Quaid again addressed the sharpshooter. "Sergeant it is Jacob! And this is the colonel's granddaughter!"

The next volley never came. An all quiet sounded. After what seemed like days, a verbal response resonated loudly. "Jacob, is it really you?"

"Yes," Quaid exclaimed. "And Sergeant, I am here with new orders!" Quaid remained calm as his eyes focused on the front door. The house was weathered. No paint covered the exterior. Large cracks came up from the foundation. An overhang shadowed the porch. On it was a single rocking chair. The front door was only a thin screen. It was dark behind the entrance. There was no movement, no light, and no sound. The roof was covered in tan shingles. It had but one chimney. However, in the heat of the summer, the stack blew no smoke. The windows were small. They were covered by shutters so that no visible line of sight was seen into the interior. Quaid waited patiently. Suddenly, the front screen burst open. A small troll-like man emerged. He stood only five foot five. He was short. He was stout. He was seemingly round as he was tall. The man came barreling down the porch stairs and across the barren yard. Despite his green hat, Quaid made out his facial features. He had big ears, and an even bigger nose. Thin, light colored eyes shone bright. His grin reached from chubby cheek to chubby cheek. His smile glowed through his grey beard which spread across his whole face. The man's physique jiggled, as his thick thighs trod down the front path. If it were December, it could have been St. Nicholas, thought Quaid. His uniform was distinct. He wore a green wool coat. The buttons were not of brass but a black rubber form. The pants were the same colored cloth. Leather gaiters covered his lower legs. At the end of his nose was a pair of wire rimmed glasses of amber. It was the military ensemble of a civil war sniper.

"Jacob!" the man cried. He tried to run toward Quaid but only moved as quickly as his heavy hind legs could carry him. Finally, Quaid and Josephine were face-to-face with the jolly old fellow. Josephine smiled at him. "Oh my Little Lady, you are beauty," he said. The man looked deep into Josephine's eyes. "And you have the colonel's green globes I see." The man then turned to Quaid. "Jacob, you have become quite the man." The Sergeant extended his hand to Quaid. He shook it firmly. "I have missed more than half your life," he said. Quaid smiled.

"Thank you Sergeant, for remembering me… and him," said Quaid.

"Remember him!" shouted the Sergeant. How could I not? The colonel was the greatest fighting man I have ever known. He saved my life on more than one occasion, and the lives of the countless others. Your father loved the men in blue. You should be proud, Jacob," he said.

"I am," said Quaid. "I am even happier to see an old friend." The Sergeant glanced over at Josephine. He took a step closer to her position and leaned in.

"So, you are the colonel's granddaughter," he whispered. "Looking at you reminds me so much of him. I am Danbeck. The Sergeant grinned, then winked at Josephine. It was if he knew all about her, and her future. Josephine politely smiled back. Sergeant Danbeck turned his attention back to Quaid. "So Jacob, why have you come?" he asked.

"I have come with a request," said Quaid. "The colonel wanted you to train his grandchild to shoot." Quaid saw a hesitation in Danbeck. "Did he not make such a request of you?" asked Quaid.

"Certainly, yes," said Danbeck. "But, she is a girl."

"Are you denying the request?" asked Quaid.

"By no means, Jacob," said Danbeck. Seemingly deep in thought, he continued. "Actually this should work to our advantage." Quaid, confused, looked deeply into Danbeck's face for clues. "Being female, she is without any prior digressions. As you know, Jacob, growing up, boys develop many bad habits in the handling of firearms. Our Little Lady here, has none. It is a clean slate," he said.

"Good then," said Quaid. "We are in agreement."

"It will be an honor to serve the colonel again," said Danbeck. Danbeck looked at Quaid, then over to Josephine. His grimace turned into a grin. Danbeck motioned with his hand toward the old farmhouse. "Come now, you both must be tired and thirsty," he said. Quaid held fast to Josephine's hand. They stepped forward in unison. Quaid felt some relief after coming to the end of their long journey. Josephine felt anticipation at the commencement of hers.

Once inside the wooden structure, Quaid entered the main room. Josephine joined him. Danbeck disappeared into the back of the house. After a time, he returned with two glasses of water. He gave the first to Josephine. He followed suit with Quaid. Danbeck walked past the two visitors and reclined in a large rocking chair. It was next to a stone fireplace. The coals were cold, and black ash filled in the surrounding space. Across the room Quaid saw a couch which could accommodate two people. It was of a framed fabric. The cloth was woven in a pattern of no particular design. It stood out in Danbeck's spartan living quarters. Quaid sat on one end. Dust lay heavily on the vacant side. Quaid let his feet rest lightly on a rectangular rug. It too was covered in a thin layer of powder. Next to the couch was an end table. It was made from a darker fiber. It held a small oil lamp. Josephine sat on a cloth covered chair. It was a faded red. Looking around, no pictures hung from the walls. No photographs adorned the cabinets, tables, or ledges, either.

It appeared to Josephine that Danbeck had no family, only the army.

Danbeck rocked back and forth for a while, then stopped suddenly. He stared long and hard at Josephine. He tilted his chair back and said, "He is in your eyes." Josephine looked over at her father not knowing how to respond. Danbeck continued as if from a self-induced trance, "'I shall see him, but not now. I shall behold him, but not nigh. There shall come a star out of Jacob.'" (Num 24:17) Before Quaid could respond, Danbeck rocked his chair forward. He addressed Josephine directly. "Little Lady, how much do you know of your grandfather?" he asked.

"Nothing," she said. "I never met him, I am sorry to say."

"Let me tell you of him then," said Danbeck. He looked over at Quaid for approval. Quaid swallowed hard, then nodded. "Very good then," said Danbeck. "The many tales I will tell. But first, let us eat."

After dinner, they remained seated at the table talking. Danbeck reached into his pocket pulling out a pipe. It had a metal shaft of an odd shape. It was of a square turned over on itself. The end was a brown oval like a barrel. The color was two-toned, the mouthpiece being black. Danbeck stuffed the barrel and with fresh tobacco. Lighting a match, he touched it to the pile of leaves. Puffing on the pipe, Danbeck created a growing orange glow in the drum, as clouds of smoke blew from his cheeks. "I still remember that day," said Danbeck. "It was the day we first met. I and two other of Berdan's sharpshooters went out on picket. Our patrol went deep into the woods. As darkness started to fall, we observed enemy movement. An entire company was headed in our direction. Our position compromised, and outnumbered, we fled. The company followed. Surrounded, we went up into the trees. Hidden from below we waited. The following day we crawled down cautiously. We made a base by an overturned weapons cart that had been stuck in the mud and abandoned. I went out to scout the enemy. Upon my return I saw a solitary man standing above my two fellow snipers. They were on the ground, bound, hand and foot. He was a tall dark gentleman dressed in Southern grey. I reached for my weapon but before I could bring it to bear he called to me.

"Fear not," said the stranger. "For I am a friend."

"Why then the restraints?" inquired Danbeck.

"I needed to control the situation; to buy some time," he replied.

"Time for what?" questioned Danbeck.

"Time to talk," he said. "My name is Matthan. My designation is Black."

"Sorry, I don't understand," said Danbeck.

"I am the emissary of President Lincoln. I am a colonel serving under General Grant," said Black.

"So you are a diplomat?" asked Danbeck.

"Of sorts," replied Black. He smiled widely, putting Danbeck at ease. Black continued, "I have come to get you out of here."

"What's the plan?" Danbeck asked.

Black walked over to a nearby tree. He reached down and pulled out his southern grey long-coat from behind it. Danbeck watched in amazement. "Some kind of subterfuge?" he asked seeing Black put on the pale garment.

"A full frontal assault," replied Black.

David Quell

"Are you mad, or just a man longing for death?" queried Danbeck.

"I assure you Sergeant, I am sane. As for death, I seek it not. Only my Creator knows when we are to meet and I merely follow down His path." Black paused as Danbeck appeared puzzled. Danbeck began to pace. "Sergeant, I am here to help. I have no intention of dying," said Black. Danbeck stopped his motion. He looked deep into the tall stranger's eyes. The green globes glowed with an ethereal light. Danbeck felt oddly comforted. He watched as Black withdrew his blade. Black moved slowly behind the snipers. With an abrupt stroke, he cut the ropes.

"Okay," said Danbeck. "Let's hear the plan."

"Good," acknowledged Black. "As I said, I will attack from the front, drawing their fire. The Confederates will speed to retaliate. This will break the ring encircling our position." Black raised his arm and pointed. "See that large stone in the center of the pasture?" Danbeck nodded. "I will take up residence there presently. Once I have established a foothold, all will break loose."

"How is that?" asked Danbeck.

"During the night, I strategically planted explosives throughout the field," said Black. "You and your boys will ignite the powder upon my command."

"How are my marksmen to find their mark?" asked Danbeck.

"I have indicated the location of each target with a small wooden cross," said Black. "Hit that designation and it will even the odds."

"As you order, sir," said Danbeck in complete understanding.

"First," said Black. "Let us have a look at this transport." He walked over to the covered wagon that was laying on its side. Black stepped onto the large broken wheel. He withdrew his Bowie knife. With a single blow, he cut open the tarp. Black spun his head around to see a large grin come over Danbeck's face. "Sergeant," he said. "Help me with this crate of heavy rifles." Danbeck approached from the other side. He pulled back the cloth to see a wooden box. Black reached down and grabbed one end. Danbeck placed his hands on the opposite point. They raised the rectangle from it's entombment. Once in the light of day, Black set it down and pulled back the lid.

"What are you doing?" asked Danbeck releasing his hold. "These are Morgan James rifles. They are good for a single stationery shot. They are not meant to be mobile. These weapons are heavy and hard to load."

"Heavy, yes," said Black. "My burden has always been so. Yet, I will shoulder it, Sergeant. I need an armory to complete this task. I can strap two to each shoulder. These rifles are quite accurate when the time is taken."

"You are a fool sir," said Danbeck.

"Maybe I am," said Black. His green eyes peered through Danbeck.. "Shakespeare once said, 'A fool doth think he is wise, but I wise man knows himself to be a fool.'"

Danbeck was pierced by the words like a spear. He regarded the man standing in front of him, knowing he was going to his death. "I understand," said Danbeck. "But why do this, sir?"

"There is no other way," replied Black. He placed his hand gently on Danbeck's shoulder. "One thing left to do now, Sergeant," he said.

"What is that, sir?"

"Pray," said Black. Black knelt his large frame down. Danbeck and his men followed. "'I will say of the Lord, He is my refuge and my fortress. My God, in Him will I trust. Surely, He shall deliver thee from the snare of the fowler, and from the noisome pestilence, Amen,'" (Psm 91:2) prayed Black. They rose. "Climb your tree, Sergeant. When you hear the sound of gunfire, make ready," said Black.

"My aim shall be true, Colonel," replied Danbeck.

Black strapped four of the forty- pound heavy rifles around his shoulders. He picked up a fifth with his right hand. He made for the edge of the woods. Black took a look back. Up in the trees, he saw the snipers perched. He turned and withdrew his Navy. Black smiled at Danbeck. "Good luck," he said. Out the shadows and into light Black ran. Black's new model revolver blazed as he went forth. The missiles drew down on the enemy, striking multiple targets in the camp. Immediately an alert sounded. On to the battlefield flowed a wave of grey, and a tsunami of minie balls. Black moved in a zigzag fashion as the projectiles burst out like popcorn. He continued the advance seeking haven behind the rock. The Confederates rushed out in response. Black dropped to one knee. He lifted his Morgan James rifle. He aimed, and fired. The lead rebel dropped as if hitting an imaginary wall. Black screamed, "Now!" He dropped his weapon and ran. Return fire came from the Confederates, unceasingly. The grey mass pushed forward, as a battery of blasts came down from the heavens. With a loud clap the footing below the army erupted. The explosions blew bodies into the air like dolls. Chaos reigned. Black's grimace converted to a grin upon reaching the rock. The ground continued to blow pieces of earth from under the grey force. It was as if the underworld had reached through the terra with its claws. Danbeck sat back against the tree's trunk to reload. It was working he thought. But as the tide had been beaten back, Danbeck heard the sound of a bugle. A thunder followed. The resounding discharge was of horses hooves hitting the hard ground. Black looked out from this fortress to see the galloping herd of the Confederate cavalry. Black stood. Heavy rifle in hand, he dropped the principal combatant. Black repeated the action in rapid succession. Having exhausted his armory of heavy weapons, Black pulled back. Danbeck's snipers added multiple strikes. One by one the riders fell to the marksmen's bullets. The remaining man rode right onto Black's position. Black fixed the shaft of the barrel with a bayonet. He retreated from the rock. Danbeck watched in shock. Black stopped and turned. He ran full speed and leapt onto the rock. Black propelled himself into the air, like a human spear. He drove the sharp point deep into the mounted rebel. The horse reared. The rider fell backwards, landing in a cloud of dust. Black's flank was now exposed. He quickly thrust himself onto the side of a passing horse. Black held tight to the neck. He placed one leg in the stirrup. The other leg he let hang. It dragged along laterally in the dirt. Black pulled hard on the mane, turning himself away from the approaching onslaught. With his free hand Black fired round after round with his revolver. The mare bore Black right off the field and back into the protection of the woods. Danbeck and the boys continued to pick apart what was left of the charge. In despair, the rebels retreated, defeated.

Sergeant Danbeck sat back in his rocking chair. Josephine, sitting on the edge of hers, waited for more. Quaid could still feel the hair standing up on the back of his neck. After several repetitive rocks, back and forth, Danbeck spoke. "Little Lady, that is why I have never listened to all the rumors. The man had a big heart. That I know. And I loved him for it." It almost seemed that a tear began to develop is in the corner of the old soldier's eye. Danbeck took a deep breath. He tried to gather his composure. Quaid looked over at the Sergeant.

"He loved you too," said Quaid. "That I know as well as I know my own name."

Danbeck directed his gaze toward Quaid. "When do we start?" he asked.

The next morning Josephine awoke under the warmth of a thick pile of blankets. She stretched each of her four limbs, all the while keeping them under the confines of the covers. A loud clamor came from downstairs. It came from the kitchen. She took a deep breath, filling her lungs with oxygen. The air traveled through the nares and stirred the olfactory sense. It was pancakes. Josephine sat up. She tried to decide which comfort would please her more, the soft warm bed or the taste of freshly grilled cakes. Hunger won out. Josephine threw back the blankets. She leapt out of bed and bounced down the stairs. Entering the kitchen she saw her father. He was facing away from her ingress. Quaid was busy turning flapjacks on the stove top. As Josephine took in the delightful aroma, Quaid turned.

"Good morning, my Beloved. The early bird catches the worm."

"Dad!" exclaimed Josephine in an embarrassing tone.

"We are alone Joey, do not worry," said Quaid.

"Where is the Sergeant?" asked Josephine

"Take a look out back," said Quaid.

Josephine strolled over to the window. She peered out into the morning sunlight. There sitting on an old tree stump was a figure dressed from head to toe in green. It was an odd site. In profile, the man held a thin long pipe in his mouth. He supported the reed handle with his hand. Puffs of white clouds rose up in unison from the glowing cauldron perched at it's end. To Joey, the bearded Sergeant looked like a leprechaun sitting on a pot of gold. "What is he up to?" questioned Josephine.

"What do you mean?" inquired Quaid.

"Why is he wearing that green uniform?" she asked.

"The Sergeant was in an elite group of marksmen during the war. It was conceived by Hiram Berdan. He was the best shot in the states. He chose the green color to give his sharpshooters camouflage during battle. Actually, he had to convince President Lincoln to commission his specialists by giving a demonstration of his abilities."

"What abilities?" asked Josephine.

"Each member of his unit had to first prove his worth by placing ten shots into a target ten inches wide from a distance of two hundred feet. Only then could you be honored with the wearing of the green," said Quaid. There was a pause as Josephine processed the information. Quaid continued. "Our Sergeant out there is the best of the best. Your grandfather knew that. He can hit a mark, dead center, at one thousand feet."

"Not possible," said Josephine.

"I have seen him do it many times during my training," said Quaid.

"You…" Josephine stuttered.

"Yes," said Quaid. "I too was his student. Now go and get ready, my Beloved. You have much to learn."

Josephine ran back up the stairs. She returned in tan pants, a blue shirt, and shoes. She smiled at her father. Then, she headed for the door. "Are you going to eat first?" asked Quaid.

"No Daddy," said Josephine. "I am too excited."

"Okay," said Quaid. "I will await your return."

Josephine turned the knob on the door. Pushing it out; the daylight came streaming in. Josephine proceeded forth. She walked slowly down to where Danbeck was sitting. He turned his head to regard her approach. The Sergeant pulled the pipe from his teeth to speak. "Little Lady, come on over and we shall commence your lesson," said Danbeck. Josephine walked right up to his position. Danbeck stood. In his opposite hand he held a long rifle. "This weapon was designed by Christian Sharps," he said. "We sharpshooters employed it in our work. It is durable, and accurate; and as you will find, a very good friend." Josephine remained still, processing the words. She understood. "I have set some targets for practice," said Danbeck. He walked towards an open field. Josephine followed. The sun poured down it's bright rays upon them. It caused Josephine to squint. The Sergeant's hat though peculiar did offer his eyes shade. It was a circular contraption. It was made from green cloth, with a leather black brim. The hat rose from his head about four inches like a pipe from a stove. Rounded at the top, it sat sagging without shape. The Sergeant reached into his side satchel. He pulled out a brown floppy cap. It seemed to Josephine to be more like a cover worn by an artist who painted in the countryside than buy a shootist. "This will keep the sun off your head," said the Sergeant. "And for your eyes…" Danbeck again reached into his sack, recovering a shaded pair of spectacles. The rims were thin metal. The lens were a light brown, almost deep orange in appearance. "Put these on, Little Lady," said Danbeck. "They will reflect the glare." As she did, the Sergeant put his own glasses upon his nose. His, like the uniform he wore, were a green; a killing green. "Now Little Lady," said Danbeck. "We begin." Danbeck directed Josephine to the shooting range. He initiated her training by going over every inch of the rifle. "This Sharps is a breech loader," said Danbeck. "It has a weight of twelve pounds. The length is forty-seven inches. It has a thirty inch barrel, and an open site. The cartridges used are .52- caliber. The shape is of a conical ball. Most can load eight to ten cartridges in the span of one minute. The breech design allows for this. The weapon is accurate up to six hundred yards." Danbeck continued with his instruction. He demonstrated how to hold, carry, clean, and stow the rifle. Josephine listened intently. She absorbed every word. She cataloged every detail. "Please come over here and lay down," said Danbeck. "I will show you to shoot the proper way. So please, Little Lady, no interruptions, no questions, or concerns."

"Yes sir," said Josephine.

Days passed, then months. Josephine became a skilled marksman. She was able to hit a target ten consecutive times, inside a ten inch circle, at two hundred yards, without fail. The following day, Danbeck led Josephine to a wooded area. "Now," he said pointing up. "You climb."

Josephine looked skyward into the tall trees. "Up there?" she asked.

"Yes," said Danbeck. "Go rest upon that fourth branch, position yourself, then draw down on the target."

Josephine began climbing. It was arduous. After a time, the little lady bird reached her perch. She sat on the limb like sitting on a swing. She readied her weapon, aimed, and fired. Josephine flew backward from her nest. She struck the ground hard. Danbeck ran to her double- time. "Are you hurt, Little Lady?" he asked with a true tone of concern.

"Only my pride," said Josephine.

"Next time Little Lady, wait for my instruction," Danbeck stated. "Now, let me show you how to brace yourself in a tree." Danbeck demonstrated how one leg should extend forward before firing. He showed Josephine how to keep the recoil from bouncing her off the branch. Josephine made no noise. She did not speak. She simply climbed the tree again and took her position. This time, she awaited instruction.

After a time, two times, and half a time, Josephine awoke early in the morning. She dressed and bounced down the stairs for breakfast. For the first time, she saw two men look up from the table. This was an odd alteration of the routine. Danbeck was always up before dawn, awaiting her on the range. Currently, he sat quietly across from her father, sipping a cup of coffee.

"Josephine it is time," said Quaid.

"Time?" she asked.

"Yes, time for us to go," said Quaid. Danbeck did not look up. He turned away from his Little Lady's gaze. He pulled back from the table and walked out of the room. "You will need to get your things together, Joey," said Quaid.

Before the stunned girl could move a muscle, Danbeck returned. He was carrying a long, thin package wrapped in cloth. "I have a gift for you, my Little Lady," he said. Danbeck handed the package to Josephine as her eyes widened. "Go ahead, open it," said the Sergeant. Josephine unwrapped the covering. It was a rifle in excellent condition. "This is a Whitworth rifle," said Danbeck. "It was a Confederate marksman's weapon. It is a bit longer, a full forty-nine inches. The barrel is thirty-three inches with a fourteen and a half inch, telescopic sight. It fires a grooved bullet. It is a muzzle loader with a percussion cap. So it needs to be cleaned constantly. It can hit a target up to eighteen hundred yards. Your grandfather procured this rifle from a southern sniper. He gave it to me as a gift. Now, I give it to you. Your grandfather had a strong sense of justice. This was his way to balance the power in a firefight. It was to help protect us." Danbeck hesitated. His head filled with memories. He smiled, ever so slightly. "The gift was from his heart. You see, my Little Lady, he loved us ordinary soldiers. This was his way of showing that love." Danbeck's speech slowed as he became gripped by emotion. He gathered himself. "That love, I confer to you."

"Thank you, my Sergeant," said Josephine. "I will treasure it, as I have my time with you."

Danbeck looked over to Quaid. "I am in your service, Jacob. Just as I was for your father," he said.

"Thank you, Sergeant. You have done your duty well."

6

The day gave way to night. The failing sun dimmed. Darkness descended on that one western town. A cooling wind blew. John Henry, the sheriff, shut the door of the jailhouse. Before returning home, he made his evening rounds. Shotgun in hand, John Henry marched methodically through town. All the buildings and shops were quiet save one. The saloon was lit up like a birthday cake. Beams of illumination spilled out of the windows, scattering radiant photons of light onto the street. Song and sounds of merriment came from within. John Henry decided to evaluate the evening's comings and goings of men. Being the town's peacekeeper, he wanted to make his presence known. He made his way up the stairs. Pushing back the double doors, John Henry crossed the barrier from black to bright. Inside the noise was loud. The clamoring of voices rose up from the ground, encircling his ears. Music added to the commotion as each key of the piano struck their cord. The barkeep was busy pouring drinks. Half empty bottles of whiskey sat open. Less full glasses of liquor scattered the remaining landscape. The bar was an abyss of disorderly mass.

In the back corner, John Henry saw a large group of onlookers gathered around one of the gambling tables. There he saw a stranger dressed in fine linen sitting with a pile of coins stacked in front of him. To his rear were two oversized cowboys. They watched intently. John Henry glanced around the game. He recognized the other card players. Johnson and Bellows were farmers. Arthur Crane was a cattleman. John Henry saw the distress in their expressions. He made his way toward their table. As he drew near, John Henry picked up on the conversation.

"I will raise you fifty," said the stranger.

"Fold," said Johnson.

"Me too," said Bellows.

Crane looked down at his cards. He held two kings and two queens. It was a good hand. However, he had not the funds available to make the bet. The stranger seemed to be able to read his thoughts.

"A little short?" asked the stranger.

"Yes," replied Crane.

"Well, I would like to make this fair for you. I do not want to win just because I have more money. So, how about you put up the deed to your land?" he asked. Crane paused. He glanced down at his hand. "In reciprocation, I will go all in with my winnings," said the stranger as he pushed the pile of coins to the center. It was more money than Crane had ever seen. The cattleman, reached into his pocket. He pulled out a pen and paper, and began to write an IOU. John Henry strode forcefully forward.

"Wait!" John Henry exclaimed. "Think about what you are doing, Mr. Crane. What good are your cattle without land?"

The stranger turned to regard John Henry. His face appeared sunken and ashen, almost grey. His countenance displayed a disdain. In his displeasure, he stood to address John Henry's interference. He glared down at the star on John Henry's chest. "Sheriff, I do not believe we are doing anything illegal here," he said smiling with sinister intent. "And may I ask, where, is the good Marshall Quaid tonight?"

"Sir," said John Henry. "Do I have a pleasure of knowing you?" he asked.

"I am the sole proprietor of the Great Circus of Helios. We have raised our tents just outside the city limits. We have come to this fine establishment to spread the word of our arrival. The circus has entertainment for the entire family," he said.

"Excuse me sir, but I did not catch your name," said John Henry.

"Where are my manners?" he queried in a laugh. "I am Adrian Mannix. I sent our permits to Marshall Quaid months ago. We are within our rights to assemble." As Mannix finished his words, the cowboys closed in on John Henry. John Henry lowered his weapon. He aimed both barrels directly at Mannix. "Just a minute," said Mannix. "We are merely engaged in a friendly game here. Let us not make judgments."

John Henry heard the click of the hammer of a handgun being pulled back from behind. His head swiveled. He turned to see Samantha standing firm with her revolver at the ready. "I hope you are not looking for trouble," said Sam.

"Now, now," said Mannix. "Is that any way for a lady to act?" he asked.

"I am no lady," said Sam.

John Henry quickly interrupted. "This friendly game, is over. I am going to politely ask all to leave," he said.

"Boys!" exclaimed Mannix. He gestured to the coins laying on the table. The two cowboys turned back. They proceeded to fill their satchels full of the loose change. "Sheriff, give Marshall Quaid my regards," said Mannix. "I look forward to our meeting."

Daybreak. On the other side of that one western town, Quaid and Josephine had arrived home. They carried their tired bodies and worn packs into the ranch house. Without a word, Josephine went directly to her room. Quaid dropped his supplies off in the kitchen. As Quaid walked toward his room, an agitation overcame him. The mental disturbance built. He attempted to calm the excitation with thoughts of peace from his youth. But instead the recollection of his father, the fire, and it's consequences, made the nervousness spread. Quaid knew it was time for him and Josephine to talk. She had now acquired great skills. But being young, she had not yet achieved wisdom. Quaid wanted to ensure that she would follow the right path. He turned and walked directly to Josephine's door. He knocked. Awaiting a response, Quaid contemplated charging Josephine to conduct herself with temperance.

"Yes Daddy?" came the query.

"I need to ask you something," said Quaid.

"What is it?" asked Josephine.

Quaid stood transfixed. He decided to wait. A better time, a better place, he thought. "Would you have a dinner with me in town tonight?" he asked.

"In town? Is it important?" asked Josephine.

"Yes it is," replied Quaid. "Later though, okay. For now get cleaned up."

"What is this all about?" Josephine questioned.

"You will know soon enough," said Quaid. "Please be patient. I need to go into town this morning. I have to speak with John Henry. I need to resume my duties. I will see you at dinner just before sundown. Oh, and, wear a nice dress."

Josephine flung open the door, a scowl crossed her face.

"See you tonight then?" questioned Quaid.

Josephine reached into her pocket and pulled out an apple. She bit down hard. "I must tend to Samson," she said as she strode past her father. Quaid peered around the corner as his little girl moved across the front entrance, closing the barrier behind. In an instant she was gone.

Dinner came way too quickly for Josephine. She sat with her father in quiet solitude for quite some time. The food had been served hot. But Josephine moved it around her plate as if it were cold. Her dress was becoming as uncomfortable as the tension in the air. The diner was not at all busy. Only two other parties were present. That was a good thing, Josephine thought. It was embarrassing enough to be seen in such attire, let alone conversing with her father. Quaid was equally apprehensive. He looked upon his beautiful little girl with love. She was all grown up. His mind flew back to the old days. He saw himself holding his little one's hand as they walked through a field of tall grass. He saw himself carrying her in his arms after falling asleep in the barn next to Samson. He saw himself sitting at the side of her bed as she slept. He smiled. Quaid recalled the hours spent with an open book, reading. Both struggled to pronounce the prose of his sacred Shakespeare. Those were happy times. Those times are gone now, he thought. That was why he had brought her to this moment. Quaid looked deeply into Josephine's big green eyes.

"Josephine, I want to tell you that I love you above all else on this earth. I always will, no matter what occurs," said Quaid. He waited for a response. None came. Quaid continued. "You are young," he said. "I would like to give you some guidance on life's journey." Still no reply. Quaid paused. He took a drink of water and swallowed. "Love God," he said. "Love God above all else. In His love, you will find strength." Quaid paused again, glancing over at Josephine. "Be kind to others. But be weary of evil. Evil looks to take advantage of the naïve and the downtrodden. Help those who cannot help themselves. You possess a great capacity for caring. Use your abilities to promote good. And always, remain principled." Quaid took another drink. "Do you understand what I am trying to tell you, Josephine?" he asked.

"Are you trying to tell me of the meaning of life?" she asked.

"In part, yes. You see, I believe the true meaning of life lies in the saving of souls," said Quaid. "The soul is God in you. He gave a great gift by placing a piece of Himself in you. You are responsible for that gift, that soul. The purpose of every life is to preserve His gift and to see that it is returned to Him with honor. That process starts with love. It began with His love for you. And the circle is completed by your love for Him. In addition, by sharing with others the news of His love, you can save more souls. Then it will be more than just the one that was given to your care. That is what I believe life is all about, my Beloved. Life is the saving of souls." Quaid held his breath, then continued. "Will you remember this?"

"I will," said Josephine softly.

"Good," said Quaid. "And may I remind you to think before you act. You have a new found power. You must be able to discern when it is appropriate to use it, and when not." Quaid displayed and expression of conviction. He continued with a tone of concern. "Some believe that strength is the ability to take a life. I believe real strength lies not in the hands but in the heart. This is the essence of our Savior's gift." Quaid looked longingly at his most beloved. "'Greater love hath no man than this. That a man lay down his life for his friends.'" (John 15:13) Quaid stopped. He could see the disquieting features form on his Beloved's face. Quaid moved quickly to defuse the situation. "Let us have no more talk of life or death. You have heard my words, now they belong to you. Do what you will."

"Very well, father," said Josephine. "I do want to tell you that tomorrow I am going over to Sam's house to help her build a new barn."

"Good for you," said Quaid. "This Is exactly what I have been trying to tell you tonight. Show all the love of God. You are generous and kind. Go show the world that kindness. Go save a soul."

The next day Josephine made the trek to the old colonel's place. Now, she thought, it was John Henry and Samantha's place. It was a bright summer day. She could feel the sun's warmth on her back. The breeze blew through the little hair that had fallen from the confines of her cap. Josephine could see farmhouse in the distance as she approached. The old barn was falling away from it's foothold. Next to it, a new building was under construction. It leaped out from the land, sprouting large beams of support up into the sky. She could see Samantha laboring in the shade of a nearby tree. Samantha appeared to be working with wood. She was sawing something, or at least trying to. Josephine rode right to the ranch, and greeted her friend. "Hello Sam, I am ready to work," said Joey.

"Thanks for coming," said Sam.

"Anything for a friend," said Joey as she dismounted and tied off Bo. Josephine walked over to the sawhorses. She looked over the situation. Samantha glanced up at Josephine.

"I am cutting a board to fit," said Sam.

"To fit?" asked Joey.

"Yes," said Sam.

"Did you measure first?" asked Joey.

"Yes," replied Sam a little irked.

"Okay, okay. Let us see if it works," said Joey.

Each took an end. They carried the wood over to the framed barn. Placing it down gently, the plank fell a little short. "Great!" exclaimed Sam, frustrated. "Now I have wasted a good piece of lumbar."

"All is not lost," replied Josephine, trying to comfort her friend. As she did, Samantha looked up, almost as a startled deer. "What is it?" asked Joey. Samantha pointed behind Josephine. Joey turned to see the figure of a man walking towards them.

He was tall, dark- haired, and appeared to have a beard. He wore a tan robe. He had no gun, or even gun belt.

"Who is that?" asked Sam.

Josephine concentrated. She drew down her gaze on the approaching phantom. After a time, she smiled. "It is Isa," she said.

"Who?" asked Sam.

"An old friend," said Joey. She raised her arm and waved. "Hello, Isa!" Joey shouted.

The young man came close, then stopped. "Josephine it is good to see you," he said.

"And you as well," said Joey. "This is Sam," she said referring to Samantha. Isa nodded and smiled. "How many years has it been?" asked Joey.

"Years?" Isa questioned.

"Yes, you know, since I last saw are you," said Joey.

"I see," replied Isa, not answering Josephine's inquiry.

There was a quiet pause. It became an uncomfortable silence. Samantha's curiosity grew. "Who are you, exactly?" Sam asked of Isa.

"' I am the good shepherd. I know of my sheep, and I am known of mine.'" (John 10:14) he said.

"So you tend a flock?" asked Sam. "Are they nearby?"

"Yes," said Isa. "I am ever present with them."

"Very good," said Sam, reassured by hearing Isa's explanation of his occupation. "We all have our calling," said Sam.

Josephine looked at Sam a little perplexed. She turned to address the young man. "Maybe you can give us a hand with the building of the barn?" asked Joey.

"I can," said Isa. "I am a carpenter at heart." Isa walked over to the freshly cut board. His hands glided over the smooth surface of the timber without a single splinter. "This will do just fine," he said.

"We have tried it already," said Sam.

"Yes, she is right," said Joey. "We did, and it did not true up."

"Have faith," said Isa. He walked the wooden beam over to the barn. He placed it down, fitting perfectly. The girls stood stunned.

"How did you do that?" asked Sam.

" ' I must work the works of Him that sent me, while it is day. The night cometh, when no man can work,' " (John 9:14) he said.

"Okay," replied Sam, somewhat uncertain of what just happened.

Josephine approached Isa. "Please, stay a while," she said. Isa smiled. He nodded in the affirmative, after which they began to work. They measured. They sawed. They hammered. They built. When the darkness came, Isa stopped. He addressed his friends, old and new.

" 'Only a little while am I with you. Then I go unto Him that sent me,' " (John 7:33) he said.

"We understand," said Joey. "You must go to attend to your herd. Thank you for your help here today." Isa smiled as he turned and walked away, for he knew more than he could say.

Another sunrise. Quaid awoke and sat still on the edge of his bed. He could feel his muscles ache. He was tired. Quaid felt a fatigue that seemed to never fade. He sat looking out of the window at the ascending sun. Quaid wondered how many more he would see. The thought did not create any melancholy.

However, the notion of separation from his Beloved did. The reflection distilled a deep despondency. Quaid veered off the emotional path he was traveling. He regained the road to reality. It was time to get moving, he thought. A new day had just begun. Quaid decided to meet it's challenges. He stood, and in his agony, he took the first step.

Entering the front room, Quaid was greeted by Josephine. "Good morning, Daddy," she said.

"Top of the morning to you," he replied. "So my Beloved, what do you have planned for this glorious day?" Quaid asked.

Just then Samantha entered the room. A wide grin decorated her face. "We are going to 'see the elephant'," she said.

In distress, Quaid turned to look directly at Josephine. "You are not going into battle!" he exclaimed loudly.

"What are you talking about?" asked Josephine.

"'Going to see the elephant', you know, going into battle," replied Quaid.

Josephine addressed Samantha. "For goodness sake, you are coming more like father every day," she said. Samantha simply smiled. Josephine faced her father. "She means we are going into town. It does not mean going into battle anymore Daddy," she said.

Quaid gave a sigh of relief. "Okay then, good," he said calmed. "Maybe I will see you there later."

"Not if we can help it," whispered Samantha under her breath. Josephine grabbed her saddlebag and Sam, sternly. She headed for the barn with both in tow.

Time hurried, but the day grew long. Josephine and Samantha had hit all the hot spots. Being two young ladies with enthusiasm, they drew a lot of attention. Some awareness was unwanted. Three cowboys under Mannix's employ took notice of the girls. Bad intentions came, as bad intentions do, from bad men. They approached the girls in an alley. Dusty, sweaty, smiles formed as they came close. Two of the cowboys were large. The third was a thin stick. He had a deep scar across his face. The wicked waif wandered right up to the girls.

"Where you headed?" asked the cowboy.

"Away from you," responded Samantha.

"Come now, don't be like that," said the cowboy. He looked over at Josephine with evil intent. "I have had my eye on you, Little Girl." The others laughed.

"Come on Sam," said Josephine. "We have somewhere to be."

"Don't leave. The party hasn't started," said the cowboy.

Josephine did not respond. She just kept walking. The cowboys, unwilling to give up on the hunt, pursued. Samantha became distressed by the stares. She did not like the way circumstances were unfolding. Agitated, Samantha stopped, and took reprisal with words. "Leave us alone, loser!"

"I am just watching, girl. And I like what I see," retorted the cowboy.

"Watch this!" exclaimed Josephine. As her assertion bellowed, Josephine drew her blade. In one smooth motion she sent it hurling through space. The cowboy jumped as the knife stuck firmly into the wall next to his head. Indignation ignited. The cowboy reached for his six shooter. As he did, an arm came down to stop his forward motion. It was the arm of the law. It was Jacob Quaid.

"I expect that would lead to trouble," said the Marshall. The cowboy looked down to see Quaid's hand firmly arresting his wrist. "I do not want any trouble, do you?" asked Quaid.

In anger, the cowboy pulled back his hand from Quaid's confinement. He gave Josephine a maniacal stare. "I will be watching you, Little Girl," he said.

The trio slowly drifted off. Quaid made his way over to the girls. He addressed them sternly. "I do not believe that was the type of excitement you should be looking for," he said. "Be more judicious when choosing to exhibit your talents. More often than not, you will find the response to force will be force." Quaid spun around. He started to walk away. He then hesitated. He looked down in remembrance. "Oh, by the way, I love you," he said. Josephine smiled in response. His declaration took some of the sting out of the scolding. "And you too, Sam," he said. Quaid smiled as he moved away. "When you two are done 'seeing the elephant', I will see you at home." Quaid made for the jailhouse with a chuckle.

7

It was Sunday, God's day. The outside of the church was of white painted wood. The entrance projected forward from the main structure. Straight on, it looked like a house within a house. The door was a brown oak. Above the door was an arched window. It was pointed at the top like a pope's mitre. On the exterior of the glass was a full cross. A large spire rose up from behind the entrance. The conical steeple sprouted from the frame in an effort to touch the clouds. Inside, planks of dark wood covered the floor. Interior lines of smooth bark walls were interrupted by stained glass. Beams of sunlight streamed through the colors creating a rainbow. The pews were short, holding only about four to five patrons. The sanctuary was recessed. It held a table for offerings. It was girded by a bright white picket. The lattice separated the parishioners from the priest.

Marshall Jacob Quaid sat still. Josephine was at his side. Both had heads hung deep in prayer. Prayers of hope, prayers of thanksgiving, and prayers for forgiveness filled the chapel.

Josephine looked every bit the lady. Her best Sunday dress was full length blue, with a lace ruffled brim at the top. It was conservative. The lines were straight, the sleeves long, and even her ankles were covered by material. The skirt fell flat from her waist. It was not fluff and lace. White buttons ran up the front. They were small and decorative. It was plain. Yet, on Josephine it was dazzling.

After the Amen, Quaid glanced around the congregation. He noticed that several citizens were not present. One was Louis McCormack. He was a cattleman. McCormack owned the largest ranch in the territory. Quaid recalled him being a permanent fixture on Sunday. Odd, Quaid thought. William Bellows, a farmer, was also noticeably absent. Bellow's land cultivated corn, wheat, and beans. His farm fed the majority of the town. He supplied food for the general store, the hotel, and the saloon. William was a regular at church. Often, he would arrive early and stay late to help with preparations and the cleanup. Bellow's presence at the chapel was perpetual. Quaid became concerned. He needed to investigate this occurrence. After the service, Quaid moved slowly from the pew to the aisle. He grinned at each passing patron. Once outside in the harsh brilliance of the sun, Quaid began to inquire. He walked directly over to Norma Tattler. Mrs. Tattler was the local busybody. If you wanted gossip, she had an endless supply. And she was happy to provide it. Quaid produced a forced smile as he approached. "Good morning," he said.

"Good morning Marshall," she replied.

"Beautiful day," said Quaid, continuing the small talk that was killing him inside.

"Yes it is," said Mrs. Tattler.

"Lovely service," said Quaid as he became even more uncomfortable.

"Yes it was," Mrs. Tattler replied.

Quaid shifted his weight. He could feel his stomach churning. He was getting nowhere. Quaid decided to throw out some bait. "I have not heard from Louis McCormack in days," he said. Quaid looked at Mrs. Tattler's face. It was still. "I usually see him at the saloon," he continued.

Mrs. Tattler took the hook and moved in closer to Quaid. She lowered her voice slightly. "I have it on good authority that Louis lost the deed to his house, his land, and his water rights." Mrs. Tattler looked around in every direction to see if anybody was listening. She then whispered, "Gambling."

"Really?" questioned Quaid trying to keep his informant engaged. "Are you sure?" he asked.

"Quite," said Mrs. Tattler.

"That is terrible," responded Quaid playing the game of gossip. "I would like to help in any way I can."

"That is what makes this whole episode so juicy," replied Mrs. Tattler. "He has just disappeared." Mrs. Tattler's eyes sparkled with excitement. She looked like a child who just found a lost toy. She continued, "Along with Mr. Bellows."

"The farmer?" asked Quaid. Lost in thought, Quaid stared into the distance. As he pondered, Josephine ran up to his position. She was a bit breathless in her haste. She stopped right in front of her father.

"Daddy, the circus," said Josephine.

"What?" asked Quaid, distracted.

"The circus!" Josephine responded more forceful, finally able to speak unimpeded. "The circus is here! Can Sam and I go?" she asked.

Quaid did not reply. He was deep in contemplation of the evanescent townsmen. His mind simply stepped aside the question. He began to drift. In a state of disconnect, Quaid glanced around for John Henry. Meanwhile, in the absence of an answer, Josephine became angered.

"Daddy!" she exclaimed loudly.

"Sorry Beloved," replied Quaid slipping away and through the crowd of churchgoers. "We will discuss this later," he shouted back. Quaid bobbed, bounced, and weaved past the body of the congregation. He ignored all inquiries as he went. At the edge of his vision, Quaid caught a glimpse of John Henry talking to Mr. Johnson. Samantha was at John Henry's side. Quaid approached quickly. Samantha saw him coming.

"Marshall, did Joey talk to you?" she asked.

"Not now young lady," retorted Quaid coarsely. "I must speak with your father." Quaid broke into John Henry's conversation. "Excuse me just a second, John," he said. Quaid tipped his hat to Mr. Johnson. "Morning Earl," he said.

"Good morning Marshall," Mr. Johnson replied.

"Have either of you seen or heard from Louis McCormack?" Quaid blurted out brashly.

"Not in days," said John Henry.

Quaid continued. "Mrs. Tattler tells me Louis lost all his money and the deed to his land, gambling."

John Henry snickered. "I did not know you ran in Mrs. Tattler's circle, Jacob," he said with some sarcasm.

"This is more than Tattler's chatter," said Quaid. "William Bellows is missing too." Before he could elaborate, Samantha spoke up.

"What about the circus, Marshall?" she asked. John Henry and Quaid glared at Samantha in disbelief. Samantha continued to bully the discourse. "Can Joey and I go or not?" she asked firmly.

Quaid hesitated. He turned toward John Henry. "How long has the circus been in town?" he asked.

"A couple of weeks," replied John Henry.

"I was there," interjected Mr. Johnson. Quaid's attention was torn in two.

"Pardon?" inquired Quaid

"I was there when Louis lost his land," replied Johnson. "It was to that Adrian Mannix."

"Who?" asked Quaid.

John Henry jumped in. "The proprietor of the Circus of Helios," he said. "I had a run in with him earlier."

Mr. Johnson continued. "Since his arrival, he has been winning gold, livestock, and even property at the gaming tables. It was not just Louis who lost, but Bellows too. Now large plots of land are under his control. He owns cattle, hogs, and chickens. He has herds of horses and one hundred cowboys at his command. With all those animals and fields, all he needs now is water."

"Water," whispered Quaid. He addressed John Henry. "Did not McCormack have some water rights?" he asked.

"Yes, of course," replied John Henry.

Quaid smelled something wicked brewing. He turned his attention back to an eager but somewhat subdued Samantha. "Sam," he said. "I do believe this is a perfect day for the circus."

Samantha smiled. She sprinted off in a hurry. "I will tell Josephine the good news," she shouted.

The afternoon sun was high. The rays sparkled off the sand like glass. The reflection formed millions of tiny stars. Each illumination produced a coronal curvature of warped waves across the grains. The effect was a succession of ocular information undulating up into a dysmorphic vision. Quaid and Josephine waited on the ridge. Sitting atop Angel and Bo, they looked out over the plain. In the distance they saw two figures approaching on horseback. It was John Henry and Samantha. Sam rode Kush. She called him that because his color was dark, like night. John Henry rode his dappled pony, Benjamin. The black beauty and grizzled bay made their way towards the two. The horses labored in the harshness of the day's light. The dust kicked up behind them leaving a buried trail of prints entombed in the dirt. Once together, the four stood on the ridge between two mountains of brass. They were as the four winds of the heavens before the Lord. And like Zechariah's chariots, they went forth into all the earth.

In the distance was the Big Top. The tall, white, tented cloth bathed in the bright beams of the day. It was Helios. The canvas was tightened by bands of twisted thick twine. The taught tentacles contracted, holding the enormous encampment earthbound. Anchored, the Big Top seemed like a city floating above the waves of heat emanating from the sands. It appeared celestial. As Quaid came close, he knew this site was far from heavenly. The front gate was constructed of large wood supports. They were held by rings of wire. A single podium stood at the entrance. It was adorned with a silken red drape. In the center was a bright yellow sun. A lone individual stood behind the stand. The four on horseback slowed to a stop. Each dismounted. They tied their rides to a hitch near the entry. Quaid walked over to the podium alone. He secured the paper passes for admittance. In silence, they walked together past the gate and into the compound. In front of the Bid Top were several large color-filled banners. They hung, and fluttered gently in the wind. Each massive design described a miraculous wonder that awaited inside. One, caught Quaid's eye. It displayed a muscular bare-fisted fighter. He was standing shirtless. He wore a metal belt, linked by leather, around his waist. Quaid tilted his head back to get a better look. He pushed his hat up to shade his vision. Beneath the figure, he saw some bold writing. It said 'The World Champion'. Below the enlarged lettering were three smaller phrases. 'Come in. Win big. Defeat the Champ'. Quaid decided to answer the invitation. He pulled back the white curtain and entered into a black hole. John Henry, Josephine and Samantha followed him into the hollow.

Inside it was dark. At the center of the darkness, several lights shone down from the sky. They flooded a raised squared stage. The platform was encircled by bands of rope. The thick twine was tethered at each corner of the square by a strong wooden beam. It was a ring. It was a ring designed solely for combat.

The four moved slowly towards the light. From the shadows strode several men. As they passed the edge of the ring, Quaid saw one man draped in a white robe. It hung from his frame like a banner. The moving collective came closer. The lead appeared to be the circus' ringmaster. He walked right up to Quaid. The other members of the gang stalled a few feet back.

The ringmaster wore a tall top hat, much like President Lincoln. He had a thin handlebar mustache, dark eyes, and shiny white teeth. His pupils appeared to radiate red. The rubescent glow accentuated the blackness emanating from inside. His attire was without color. His waistcoat was with tails. There was but a single splash of white for a shirt. He had no handgun. Taking off his top hat, the ringmaster inquired, "Marshall Quaid, can I help you?"

"I have come with my girls for the show," replied Quaid, glancing back at Joey and Sam.

"The first bout does not start for several minutes," said the ringmaster. "You are welcome to stay and watch our champion warm up." The ringmaster turned his head in the direction of the fighter standing stalwart in his white robe. The fighter glared at Quaid with disgust. He thrust his fist into the palm of his other hand.

"Easy," said Quaid. "You will get your chance soon, I am sure."

Out of the black of the pit echoed a loud voice. "Why not now Marshall?"

Quaid and his companions looked up. Quaid was irritated by the insinuating speech. "I fight for justice, not for sport," he shouted.

"How about a small wager, then, Marshall?" asked the voice. Before Quaid could reply, he continued. "I will donate one hundred dollars for food, medicine, and supplies, for your one western town's poor. That is, if, you can defeat the champion."

"Certainly not," replied Quaid. "As I said, I do not fight for sport. And definitely not for money, or a bribe."

"I understand," said the voice. "You are afraid. I guess the apple does not fall far from the tree."

Quaid's fervor shook. He held fast, still in control. Quaid shouted back. "If I am the fearful party, why do you hide in the shadows?" No answer came. Quaid continued. "Come down here so I may meet you face to face."

Another group of thugs appeared on the other side of the ring. They moved forward in unison. The mass of men came concealing a single individual in the center. The cluster stopped, then separated as a fan. A well-dressed gentleman stepped away from the hive. "Good day Marshall," he said. "My name is Adrian Mannix."

"Why is it I do not know your name?" questioned Quaid.

"What is a name?" asked Mannix.

Quaid scowled, visibly disturbed by the remark. Suddenly, the remainder of the lights came up. The surrounding stands were now lit with the same resplendence as the ring. Quaint could see people filing into the seats like bees to honey. The ringmaster could now be seen in the center of the square. He held a large microphone in his hand. The ringmaster addressed the audience by belting out a greeting. "Welcome ladies and gentlemen! We have a special treat for you today at the Great Circus of Helios. It is a battle of titans. It will match the world champion versus your own defender of the people, Marshall Jacob Quaid!" A great roar rose from the crowd. As it did, Quaid spun around. He saw the multitude staring directly at him. "To the victor goes one hundred dollars in gold coin earmarked for your one western town's poor!" shouted the ringmaster. An eruption of applause left Quaid stunned.

"It is your move, Marshall," said Mannix to the stationary Quaid.

John Henry grabbed Quaid's shoulder firmly, drawing his attention. "You do not have to do this, Jacob. Let me go in your stead," he said.

"I have seen my fair share of bullies and bad guys. This one is no different," said Quaid. "Besides, he is not that big. I can take him." Quaid turned toward the girls. "Josephine, since I will be occupied, you must deliver the package to the destination."

"You mean take the gold to the treasury?" Josephine asked excitedly.

"Yes," said Quaid in a whisper. He pulled the young lady aside. "With the whole town here, you will be able to slip away in obscurity."

"I know I can do this, Daddy," said Josephine.

"You will need help," said Quaid. "How about John goes with you?"

"I will take Sam," she said smiling.

Quaid looked over at Samantha. She had an absurd grin on her face. Quaid shuttered. "Fine," he replied in reluctance. "Just be careful."

The ringmaster's voice broke the ambient chatter. "And now, ladies and gentlemen, here is our champion, the undefeated king of the ring, Orcus!" A bright spotlight exploded, illuminating not a man but a gargantuan. He had wild red hair. And he bore a full beard. His eyes were sunken. One could see his grey skin was covered by knots and boils, as he was bare to the waist. His form was chiseled and muscular. The lower half was covered by black tights. High laced boots lay at the bottom. Quaid stared at the marauder. As the giant entered the ring, Quaid thought that he could be as much as six cubits tall. Quaid turned to catch John Henry's eyes. They were wide. Mannix headed for his ringside seat. As he did, Quaid shouted back at him. "I thought I was to fight your champion?" inquired Quaid, referring to the man in the white robe.

"Orcus is our champion," Mannix replied.

John Henry clasped Quaid by the arm, restricting his motion. "Stop this Jake! It is a set up," he said.

Quaid faced John Henry. " I know. But the whole town is here, and the people are hungry," said Quaid.

"Come now Jake, he is massive," said John Henry.

"You know what they say," said Quaid. "The bigger they are…"

"The harder they hit?" injected Samantha. Josephine giggled.

"Not funny," replied an angered Quaid. "Now you two get going before I change my mind." Josephine and Samantha moved out quickly. Neither turned to look back.

Orcus strode to the center of the square. Quaid reached up and grabbed the ropes. He hoisted himself into the ring. Quaid looked down at John Henry. He nodded in the affirmative. Quaid slowly walked forward. He stopped in front of the ringmaster. "This match is set for twelve rounds. Winner by knockout only!" the great orator announced. A deafening yell resounded from the crowd. Quaid leaned in and whispered to the ringmaster.

"What are the rules?" he asked.

"There are no rules," replied the ringmaster. "This is a street fight."

The bell rang. Orcus immediately charged Quaid. He raised his imposing arm out like the branch of the tree. The rumbling lumber clipped Quaid across the chest, knocking him on his back with a thud. A scattering of disapproving booing arose from the audience. Quaid quickly shook out the cobwebs. He rolled and reached his feet. Quaid put some distance between himself and the giant. Orcus again drew down on his prey. He swung high and hard. Quaid ducked under the blow. He responded with a strike to Orcus' abdomen. No effect. The giant's other arm came around, again striking Quaid. Hit hard, Quaid fell. This time Quaid scurried to his corner on his hands and knees.

"Jacob, you cannot stand toe to toe with this behemoth!" shouted John Henry. "You must use your speed. Strike and move. Strike and move."

"Good advice," said the breathless Quaid, gasping for air.

Quaid turned back to his opponent. He started to circle the titan. Quaid darted in close, then landed a kidney punch. No result. Quaid spun around to the front. Orcus swung and missed. Quaid countered with a barrage of body blows. In and out he went, jabbing the giant. Orcus opened his stance. Quaid lead with a strong uppercut to the gut. His hand bounced back like opposing polls of a magnet. Orcus grabbed Quaid, lifting him up like a doll. He squeezed with the power of ten pythons.

The bear hug forced oxygen from Quaid's lungs. His body began to go limp.

"I will crush you like a bug. Then feed you to the fowl," said Orcus with dread.

The crowd screamed, encouraging Quaid. With the little life he had left, Quaid drew back his arms overhead. He then thrust them forward, and smashed his palms firmly over the ears of Orcus. The beast howled. His razor claws cut Quaid's shirt to shreds as he dropped Quaid's feeble form. The Marshall crashed to the canvas in a bloody heap. Liquid red poured from the cutaneous rents. Orcus raised his hands to cover is ears for a few seconds, as the pain seared through his drums. Orcus'anger intensified. He strode forward toward Quaid. He still lay unmoving. With brute force, Orcus kicked Quaid in the gut. It sent the Marshall hurling across the ring, He landed a few feet from his corner. Orcus approached. He stood over Quaid's broken body in insolence. "You are no son of Black," he said. "You are weak flesh." With that, Orcus spat on the vanquished Quaid. The monster moved slowly off to his corner.

Quaid was enraged. His blood boiled. The burning heart in his chest beat with a fervid fury. In execration, Quaid desired to rip the organ from it's cage. He stood defiant. Quaid released a piercing scream as he tore the tattered shirt from his body. The shriek was so violent it shook the angels. Orcus, hearing the cry, spun back around. Blood dripped from Quaid's wounds onto the mat. The Marshall wiped his mouth. His eyes glazed over. Sanity slipped his mind. With his stained hand, Quaid painted a cross upon his chest. The crucifix wept, leaving a trail of sanguineous tears. "I will not yield!" he yelled.

"You believe that you are saved. You are not," responded Orcus in an epithetic retort.

Quaid released his belt buckle. He rapidly removed it from his waist. Quaid wrapped the leather band around his hand. The metal fastener faced out. Orcus rushed him. Quaid attacked. Orcus swung wildly. Quaid eluded the thrust. From a subordinate station, Quaid hammered a metal fisted strike to the side of his knee. Orcus immediately dropped down, unable to support his weight on the injured appendage. Quaid crushed the joint with a quick kick. Quaid accelerated his mass, landing full force upon Orcus' jaw. While he was immobilized, Quaid unraveled the belt from his hand. He leapt over Orcus, hooking a noose around his neck. Quaid leaned backward and with all his might, pulled. The beast struggled to breathe. Quaid tightened the tether by placing his foot on the demon's back, then straightening his leg. Orcus thrashed with a savage anger. His talons tore at Quaid's trousers, splitting the fibers. Quaid fixed his grip, strangling his foe. Quaid's agonizing cry became a shrill. His muscles continued to contract, creating a twitching tension. Orcus' oxygen depleted. All color drained from his face. He fought for air. Gasping, Orcus reached his hands for the snare. Quaid's intensity increased.

"Stop! Jake stop!" yelled John Henry. He rushed on to the mat. "Jake, you are killing him!" Quaid persisted, undaunted. John Henry shackled the beast's hands in chains. "It is over Marshall," shouted John Henry.

Quaid slowly returned to the living. He let go his grip. Unconscious, Orcus' carcass fell flaccid. Quaid stood. His suffering swelled. Quaid held out his hands and clenched his fists. From his laborious misery Quaid erupted in torment. His wail resounded. Disgusted; Quaid spat on the motionless monster. John Henry placed himself between the Marshall and the giant. "I said, it is over," John Henry reiterated loudly. "Go home my friend. I will handle the details," he said calmly. Exhausted, Quaid relented. He left the arena battered and bruised. Walking out, Quaid hung his head in humility. But the embers of his rage still burned.

8

On the other side of town, far from the towering spires of the tents, a solitary wagon waited. It sat in silent stillness. There was no parade. No fanfare. The wheeled transport was drawn by six sleek steeds. The horses were hitched and at the ready. The two at the point began to paw the ground in anticipation. A quiet breeze blew. It seemed to soothe the animal's apprehension. The golden sun shone streaks of lemon from out of the clouds. They radiated the sand in a bright, buttery pigment. The color was as the coach's cargo. The precious metal was loaded. The freight was now ready for conveyance.

The carriage was a Concord. The original maroon was now browned by years of wind, sun, and sand. The yellow wheels were spoked. The front set was smaller than the back. The side panels were of varied sizes and shapes. But all were of one color. Tan canvas curtains hung from the windows. Atop the stage was a small Iron ring to secure packages. Below, the thorough braces were leather. The strapped suspension allowed the cart to teeter from side to side. During motion the compartment rolled back-and-forth like a baby's bassinet. The rear boot was black, as was the front. These polished cloths held cargo if needed. On the right side of the driver's box was a long handled brake. The apparatus extended out like an executioner's lever. Josephine and Samantha walked out of the dispatch door. Josephine reached to grab the stage. She turned the handle and began to open the egress.

"I thought you would drive the team," said Sam.

"No," replied Joey. "Besides, you are better with a whip," she said smiling. Sam scowled. "Rider's up!" Josephine hollered. Sam relented. It was three full steps to secure her seat on the bench. She lifted her foot, elevating her leg. Sam slowly made the climb. She steadied the ascent with her right hand. In her left, she held a Winchester yellow boy. Once situated, Sam placed the rifle on the bench next to her position. Still slightly irritated by Josephine's barb, Sam did not look back before she grabbed the reins. With a powerful roar, Sam yelled, "Ho!"

The team took to a trot. All six struggled against their collars, dragging the wagon through the dirt. The heavily harnessed horses drew the coach away from the station. Sam could feel the brawn beneath her legs, leveraging influence on the carriage. The string's strength shook the stage with each stride of flowing forward force. A current was created as the wagon picked up speed. It moved quickly out of town, and on to the trail. The air thrust Sam's hair back. She pushed her hat down firmly on her head, securing the cover. As she drove, the dark locks fell from beneath the brim. The wind stung her face. Traveling down the path, Sam remained alert. She thought, 'Be sober, be vigilant. Because, your adversary, as a roaring

lion, walketh about, seeking whom he may devour.' (1 Peter
5:8)Her eyes scoured the landscape. Alert ears readied up. The
only perception was a little more than a zephyr. Sam's olfactory
system analyzed each odor. The savory suggestion of the team's
perspiration gave the sense of a slight stench. Sam's slightly
moistened mouth tasted the dry dust of the trail that was kicked
backward by the galloping equestrians. The trail was torturous
and long. It was a half day's ride to the home station. Sam drove
the horses hard, hoping to arrive before the loss of light. The
churning wheels rolled the box along at an alarming rate. Inside
the coach, it was calm. The sun continued to pour out waves
of white rays, drowning the chariot. The day grew hot. Sweat
dripped down the front of Sam's face like tears. It mixed with
the dirt, muddying her features. Sam knew the importance of
her task, and her cargo. She was determined to see the gold got
to it's destination. Sam pushed on with a steadied perseverance.

After hours of rough travel through the open prairie, the
stage approached a narrow pass. The breath of the road seemed
to constrict. The dwindling width stretched out into a gorge
lying between two mountainous forms of earth. The path would
place the coach in a box for a time. And Sam knew it. She slowed
the horses to a walk. Sam looked ahead with diligence. She
turned her head from side to side, then full around. There was
a hush. Nothing appeared amiss. She continued on. Halfway
through the chasm, the team became agitated. Sam wondered
what spooked the animals from their paces. Over her shoulder
they came! A pack of thieves on horseback approached fast.
Sam realized what came next. It was on! With a lash of the
whip, Sam roused the lines to top speed. The sound of the

hooves hitting the ground, beat like a tom-tom. The rhythm quickened. The rate of the race heightened. Both bandits and beasts strained to outrun and overtake. The cowboys spurred their mounts right up to the driven dust of the wagon wheels. Two came along starboard. They ran parallel. Another crept in behind. The chase cowboy leapt. He landed on to the triangular pouch of the boot. With stealth, he moved forward. Sam sensed his presence. The force of his landing had jerked the stage. She grabbed her rifle. With a quick pivot she turned. Sam placed one boot on the bench. Her finger touched the trigger. She pulled. The blast blew her back. Sam stumbled. The projectile missed the intended target. The bandit ducked for cover. Sam sat up. She grasped her Bowie knife. Sam raised her hand. She slashed the leather band that bound the bags. The torn tether released them from their restraint. The cases bounced backward in reverse. The packages crashed over the cowboy like a wave, pushing him from his perch. Simultaneously, the parallel riders sprung. They landed solidly. The wagon rolled. Their weight drew down the side. The carriage rebounded, as Sam slid off balance. The cowboys crawled forth like spiders. The quarters became close. Sam stepped up and out the opposite side. She vaulted to the port, like a javelin. At her apex, she spun. In the axis of rotation, Sam pulled both pistols from their sheaths. She fired as she fell. Sam emptied every chamber. The bullets riddled the coach. Each explosion burst. The rupture released numerous chips and splinters. The cowboys were struck. The eruptive energy repelled the enemy. The bandits hurled through the air. Sam hit the ground with a thud. The impact knocked the wind from her lungs. The stage powered ahead at higher speed. The last two cowboys approached the transport. The bandits rode rough. Their locomotive mass pounded up and down violently. The velocity of the runaway vehicle increased. The wheels spun faster and faster. The horses ran wild. The animal's anxiety fueled the frenzy. The wagon veered off the path. On an angle, the cowboys came in close. The men made the leap. Both landed square. Each held firm. Their grips tightened. The rampaging horseflesh raged on. Pulsations of pressurized work percussed across the coach. The undulations waft the bandits bodies back and forth. Their forms were flung to and fro. After a time, each steadied his stance. The lead clasped the handle to the door. Forcing it down, he opened it. A great roar arose. The howl was promptly followed by a thick clawed paw. The muscular limb contacted the cowboy. It drew him inside with extreme prejudice. Screams and splashings of red spread through the air. The drapes became a canvas of ruby droplets. The door was drenched in a pattern of death. The last cowboy, now covered in his comrade's blood, moved to evade the deadly arm's attack. He leapt, eluding the giant appendage. The bandit hit the ground hard. In a state of confusion, the cowboy looked up from his fall. He saw a visage with exposed white fangs. It was Samson. In defiance, the beast released a deafening wail.

The rudderless ship careened out of control. The speed continued to build. The stage was now on a direct line to a large precipice. Samson had protected the cargo. The coup was crushed. But now the mammalian martyr was drawn to certain death at the mountain's edge. Samantha recovered, she stood up strong. She saw the wagon racing towards destruction. Hope left her heart. In angst, she whispered to the Lord. "'O turn unto me, and have mercy on me. Give thy strength unto thy servant, and save the son of thine handmaid.'" (Psm 86:16) As the words ascended to heaven, Sam's spirit filled with sadness.

A loud bang broke through the desperation. From a distance, a shot blew down off the peaks like an eagle. It struck the hitch of the stage. The bullet blasted the connection, causing a separation of team and trolley. The coach slid. The resulting torque tossed the Concord onto its side. The full weight of the wagon crashed into the dust. A flume of powdered soil burst forth from the earth, covering the fallen convoy. The stage stopped. Samantha's line of sight traced the path of the shell back to it's origin. The retrograde view revealed a familiar figure. It was Josephine. On the mountain top she stood strong against the sun's light. Her shadow cast an imposing image over the elevation. From the summit, Josephine raised her Whitworth rifle high. Samantha smiled at the sight of her sister. She waved in recognition. All was well.

Back at home, Quaid waited by a warm fire. The flames felt like a soothing balm to his sore muscles. Quaid sat in comfort, yet it was difficult for him to relax. His mind was overwhelmed with worry. The reflection lit up his hippocampus like a nova. After his day in the ring, Quaid wondered what possible peril Josephine and Samantha had faced. He had to trust in their teachings. He had to believe they were prepared to drive that stagecoach. Quaid dropped to his knees. He prayed. "' I pray for them. I pray not for the world, but for them thou hast given me. For they are thine.'" (John 17:9) Quaid returned to his chair. He trusted in the Lord. However, as the hours grew long, his anxiety did the same. Finally, Quaid heard the approach of riders. His perception peaked. The sound of two on horseback resounded in his ears. Quaid got to his feet. He walked over to the window and glanced out. The barn door was ajar. A flickering light emanated from within. After an eternity, two shapes emerged from the arcane black. Quaid withdrew from the window. He sat back down. The front door flung open. Josephine and Samantha stepped inside. Quaid smiled, exaggerating the age lines driven into his face. Josephine looked directly at her father. He appeared weary. "Hello father," she said.

"Hello Beloved," he replied.

Samantha gave a smirk. "Good evening, Marshall," she said.

"Yes, yes it is," said Quaid. "You girls have any trouble?" he asked.

"A bit of a rough ride, but nothing out of the ordinary," said Josephine.

"Really?" inquired Quaid.

"Just a few bumps and bruises," said Josephine.

"Looks like you have a few bumps of your own," said Samantha snidely. "No matter, they will heal, won't they?" said Sam.

Quaid grimaced. "Would you like to sit by the fire for a while?" he asked Josephine.

"Sure!" exclaimed Sam, dropping down on the couch like a wet load of laundry. Despite an alternate desire, Josephine relented and sat.

"So tell me about the trip," said Quaid.

"Not much to tell," replied Josephine.

Quaid looked over at Samantha. "Anything to add?" he asked.

"The gun play was exquisite!" Sam blurted out.

Quaid became uneasy. He straightened his reclined posture. "What does this mean, Josephine?" questioned Quaid.

"As your Shakespeare once said, it is much ado about nothing," Joey replied.

Quaid burned inside. Samantha added fuel to the flames. "I wouldn't call a firefight, nothing," she said.

"A firefight?" Quaid inquired angrily. "What happened out there Josephine?"

"As I said father, nothing to report. Sam is just pulling your leg," said Joey. "Now if the inquisition is over, I am going to wash up," she said sternly. With that, Josephine stood and walked into the kitchen. Left alone, Quaid turned his intense gaze at Samantha. She simply stared back with a silly smile.

"Always ready with a quip?" Quaid asked of Samantha.

"I like to turn a phrase now and then," she said.

"Some say sarcasm is merely a means to conceal one's true feelings," said Quaid. "Are you hiding something from me, Little Miss?" he asked.

Sam fumed. "What do you think I am hiding?" she asked in irritation.

"I did not say you are not trustworthy. I only mention that I can sense your pain, even if you think no one can," replied Quaid.

"What do you know of pain, Marshall?" Sam asked angrily.

"I know sorrow," said a consoling Quaid. His eyes met hers with understanding. "I have lost a loved one, or two. It still hurts to this day," continued Quaid.

Samantha squirmed in her seat. Her face became flush. Her eyes glazed. Her respirations quickened. Quaid took notice. "It is your parents. Is it not, Sam?" he asked. A single tear formed in Samantha's eye. Try as she did, Samantha could not hold it back. The droplet ran down her cheek, moistening her face. Samantha turned away her bearings.

"Sometimes it hurts so much, I feel like my heart will burst from my chest," she said sadly.

"I know Little Miss," said Quaid. "The suffering, unfortunately, will never stop. It is a relentless torment. It is the kind that consumes a small piece of you every day." Quaid looked lovingly at his Little Miss. He continued. "Sam, love can ease the loss," he said. "Let me be the first to give you hope." Quaid stood and walked across the room. He picked up a small wooden box. It was engraved with a cross. Quaid made his way over to Samantha. He sat down on the couch next to her.

"What is that, a music box?" she asked.

"It is the almsgiving of my father," said Quaid. "A gift of charity and love, and I would like you to have it." Samantha wiped away the tears. She held the box gently in her hands. Samantha stared fondly upon the cross garnishing the top. "My father always told me to think of him whenever I saw the cross. It represents his love for me, just as it does our Lord's love for us. As long as you hold that in your heart, no amount of pain can overcome you," said Quaid.

Samantha slowly raised the lid. Inside was a metal cross. "What is this?" she asked. The crucifix appeared blackened on the edges as if having been through fire.

"It was my father's," replied Quaid. "It was all that was left of him in the ashes. He wore it always with honor. He modeled his life in the duty of this symbol. And above all he loved it's meaning with all his heart. I am giving it to you so that you may know that love." Samantha gave a subtle smile as she placed the cross around her neck. As she went to close the box, she noticed a false bottom. Samantha lifted out the divider. Below she saw a small scrap of paper. Quaid saw her inquisitive expression. "Go ahead, read it," said Quaid.

"'God gave us a spirit not of fear but of power and love,'" (2 Tim 1:7) said Sam softly.

Quaid gently held Samantha's hands in his. "My father always reminded me of the power of love. I wanted you to know that you are loved my Little Miss. The cross will remind you. Samantha gave a grin. She leaned over and hugged the Marshall. "Also know this my Little Miss," said Quaid. "True strength lies not in the hands but in the heart."

"Yes, you are right, Marshall," said Sam.

9

Quaid awoke early that morning. He had trouble sleeping. Bad dreams had disrupted his slumber. Quaid drank his third cup of coffee while he recalled the night before. Spiders. It was spiders. They were large. Some were larger than Quaid's head. They came out of the walls. Their four pairs of ocelli deflected the light like death. Their color was dark as a pit. Their fangs hung down below the chelicerae. Their rounded hourglass figures held venom and enzymes to poison, then liquefy their prey. Their eight legs were segmented. Hydraulic pressures extended the limbs of the exoskeletons, creating motion.

The arachnid army approached Quaid fast. Coming from ceiling and floor, they scurried. Quaid was spellbound by the multitude. His anxiety heightened. It was not from fear. It was the natural human aversion to the insect. The detestation created a bitter taste sensation in the back of his throat. The horde advanced. They consumed the walls, covering every available space. The greatest of them ran up the facade to Quaid's left. It leapt. Quaid's reflexes deployed. He raised his arm. Quaid's enormous hand clasped the spider in flight. In a rage, he clenched his fist, violently expressing coelomic fluid across his face. Quaid stirred. Fully aware of his surroundings, he contemplated the dream. It was only an aberration. The memory soon left his mind.

A new dawn had just begun and Quaid had to make for town. A beautiful day unfolded in front of him as he rode. Angel made the trip easy. Quaid was comfortable on her back. He was serene. The sight of the rising sun on the trees softened the terrors of the night. Quaid smiled seeing the hues of pink, orange, and blue, on the horizon. Life seemed simple. Life seemed good. At the jailhouse, Quaid got right to work. He sat behind his desk and put pen to paper. A public office always involved record keeping. Quaid began to immerse himself in thought. A knock at the door broke Quaid's concentration. "Come in," said the Marshall. The door blew open. In walked Adrian Mannix. He was flanked by five husky ranch hands. Their mass filled the room. Quaid, surprised, glared out at them from behind the desk. Mannix quickly moved forward, pressing against the edge of the bureau.

"Good morning, Marshall," he said.

"What is this about?" inquired Quaid.

"I think you know," said Mannix. He continued. "You blocked my access to the water rights. The bank stopped the foreclosures on the land I need. And you took two of my men into custody."

"It is all very legal," responded Quaid with a quip.

Mannix pounded his fist firmly upon the desk. He leaned in close. "You do not know who you are dealing with Marshall," he shouted in anger.

"Educate me then," said Quaid sternly.

"I plan to, choirboy," said Mannix. A sense of dread overcame Quaid. He reached for his weapon. Before Quaid could pull his pistol from its sheath, five firearms were drawn and directed at him. "Don't be a hero. Heroes die," said Mannix. "You have become intolerable, choirboy," he said. "I aim to end your interference." Mannix straightened his posture. He walked over to the window and glanced out. The street was clear. He turned his attention back to Quaid. "I believe you now know who I am, choirboy," said Mannix. He paused. Mannix fixed his eyes angrily on Quaid. "You fool, I am eternal!" he exclaimed with a ferocious wrath. "Do you really think you can defeat me?"

Quaid lowered his head. "No," he said softly. "Maybe, not." The Marshall's strength seemed to waver. Mannix grinned in triumph. Quaid sat quietly for a time. The silence was broken when Quaid reared his head in defiance. "I do not have to defeat you," he said firmly. "One has already done so."

"What!" screamed Mannix, enraged. "I will see that you suffer, choirboy!" shouted Mannix. He motioned to his minions. "Lock him up!" he cried. Mannix followed as the cowboys led Quaid to his cell. The Marshall gave no resistance as he walked into the barred detention. The door slammed closed. Quaid turned and faced Mannix with determination. "Let us see how you like being confined, choirboy," said a smug Mannix.

"'For I am persuaded, that neither death, nor life, nor angels, nor principalities, nor powers, nor things to come, nor height, nor depth, nor any other creature, shall be able to separate me from the love of God, which is in Christ Jesus our Lord,'" (Rom 8:38) said Quaid. Mannix fumed.

John Henry awoke early that morning. The Marshall was not the only soul up at daybreak. John Henry was a man of discipline. His adherence to order had served him well. Now it was habit. That day, John Henry traveled into town for supplies. As usual, he completed his tasks with efficiency. Therefore, John Henry had extra time allotted for frivolity. He decided to call on his old friend, the Marshall. John Henry strolled along the boardwalk casually. He looked briefly into the various shops and businesses located along the main street. John Henry reached the jailhouse sporting a carefree spirit. He peered into the barred window. John Henry was expecting to see his friend hard at work. His easy demeanor was startled by the vision of several armed men. He counted six in total. Five had their weapons trained on the Marshall. John Henry stood in shock as the cowboys led the Marshall to the back of the jailhouse. A strong fear welled up inside him. John Henry jumped back against the outside wall of the structure as not to be detected. He looked left, then right. Panic ensued. It peeled through his skin like carving the layers of an onion, and drove deep into his soul. No one had observed this action however. Frantically, John Henry made his way back to the rig. He climbed aboard the wagon. With a whip of the reins, he rolled the flatbed right out of town. Once in the countryside, John Henry pushed the horses hard. He needed help and he needed it fast. John Henry drove the tandem to physical exhaustion. He ran the beasts to the limits of the carriage's framework. In haste, he halted the crew in front of the Marshall's home. At the top of his lungs, John Henry screamed. "Joey! Joey are you home?" There was no reply. He cried out over and over. Each burst erupted with increasing reverberation. "Joey! Joey!"

Bang! Bang! Bang! John Henry heard a barrage of gunfire. It came from the back of the house. He sprinted towards it's origin in horror. John Henry pleaded not to let him be too late. "'Thou hast heard my voice. Hide not thine ear at my breathing, at my cry,'" (Lam 3:56) he whispered as he ran. John Henry sped around the corner of the dwelling with revolver drawn. Lying on the ground he saw Josephine with her Whitworth in hand. Next to Josephine was his Samantha. She held a rifle as well. Being hurried, John Henry did not take notice of the shooting range the girls had erected. As more shots rang out, John Henry dropped flat to the ground. His body hit the turf with a tremendous thud. Ducking for cover, he shouted, "Get down!"

The girls turned their heads to see John Henry flop like a pancake. They giggled at his dramatic display. "Nice dive Daddy," shouted Samantha jokingly. "But Joey and I are just taking target practice." The laughter grew louder as an embarrassed John Henry stood to brush the dirt from his clothes.

"Girls," he said. "Stop this, I have serious news." The two siblings sat up attentively. John Henry continued. "Josephine, your father is being held captive by Adrian Mannix."

"Where?" asked Josephine.

"At the jailhouse," replied John Henry.

Josephine stood resolute. She felt the terra firmly underfoot. Samantha followed suit. With empowerment, Josephine addressed John Henry. "We must mount a rescue now."

Samantha looked directly at her sister. "What's the plan?" she asked.

Determination filled Josephine's face. "John Henry, ready the covered wagon," she said in a commanding tone. "And prepare the weapons, and explosives."

"Certainly," said John Henry.

"The sooner we move, the greater our advantage," said Josephine. She turned to Samantha. "We will need more than guns," she said. "Samantha, let us go to Sampson. He will again, defend us." Josephine and Samantha ran to the barn. As Josephine pulled open the door, the light poured into the darkened interior. The beams reflected off the piles of hay on the floor, illuminating the soft flaxen strands of straw. In the center of the mounds of thatch lay Samson. Josephine made her way over to him. She knelt down and stroked his fine fur. "My boy, we need you," she whispered lovingly. Josephine stood. She signaled her champion to stand. He followed her decree. Samantha smiled in anticipation.

The wagon rolled into town. It moved slowly from the main street to an alley behind the jail. John Henry sat alone atop the buckboard. He drove the rig with a calm intent, as not to draw attention. Coming to a conjunction of backstreet and roadway, John Henry stalled the transport. It stood still. Josephine pushed back the rear covering. She crawled out quietly. Josephine made her way around the schooner towards the rear of the cells. She kept her hat low, covering her features.

At the corner of the building, a cowboy stood watch. He saw Josephine approaching, her head pointed towards the ground. The morose posture caught the eye of the gunfighter.

"Hey you there!" he shouted. Josephine stopped dead. The cowboy closed on the sullen figure with his pistol drawn. "What is your business here?" he asked. Josephine remained silent. "Let me see your face!" he demanded. Josephine raised her head, revealing a colored kerchief across her features. The cowboy pointed his gun at her. He reached over to pull down the veil. With one motion, the cover came free. Under the cloth was a toothy grin. Shocked to see the Marshall's daughter, the cowboy gasped. Before he could call for help, the butt of a rifle struck him from behind. His limp body dropped to the dirt like a drape. Unveiled was a smiling Samantha. She winked at her sister in acknowledgment. It was on.

Samantha hustled over to the barred window of the Marshall's cell. She bent slightly. Samantha signaled Josephine to take a step up. Josephine placed her foot in Samantha's hands. The sturdy Little Miss lifted her right up to the window. Josephine peaked in. The chamber was dark. Through the dusk, she could see her father sitting on a cot. He appeared unharmed. "Daddy," she whispered. Quaid looked over his shoulder. He saw Josephine's pretty face bobbing between the bars.

"Joey, what are you doing?" inquired Quaid.

"Dad, no time to talk. Just stand back, and get ready to run," she replied.

John Henry carried a barrel of gunpowder over to the wall. Josephine dropped down from her roost and ran. Samantha scurried to steady the horses. Josephine raced to the back of the wagon. John Henry struck a match and lit the fuse. Marshall Quaid took his blanket and kneeled in the opposite corner. He covered himself with the cloth. Boom! The blast burst open the stone stockade, reducing it to rumble. Quaid was pelted with debris. Dropping the cover, he saw a large jagged hole in the wall. Quaid hurried through the gateway to safety. Josephine saw her father emerge from the eruption. She smiled with relief. Knowing it was not yet over, Josephine shouted forcefully, "Sampson protect!" The bear gave out a loud roar. He ran forth full throttle. His four paws pumped like the pistons of the steam engine. Without hesitation the beast ran directly into the breach. His large frame disappeared into the darkness. As the waves of the explosion shook the floor from the back of the jailhouse, Mannix made his escape via the front door. At the edge of the exit, he turned to his hired guns.

"Find Quaid! End this!" Mannix shouted.

The men rushed to the back of the jail. There they were confronted by an enraged carnivore. Outside of the compound, Josephine heard the wailing and gnashing of teeth. Her heart was heavy. She feared for her loved one's welfare. Shots rang out through the tumult of the scuffle. Each pop sent a shuttering, shaking cold through Josephine's soul. Mannix dashed out the doorway. Waving his arms, he directed his crew of cowboys to take up their positions. "To your stations!" he yelled. The men scattered like rats. Mannix mounted his horse. He spun his ride around to face the armed company. With an indignant ire, Mannix reared his head. "Take skin for skin!"

Josephine sped to the front of the wagon to join Samantha. Looking back, she saw her father stumbling. He was still dazed from the blast. John Henry tried to steady his friend. With John Henry's help, Quaid managed to crawl into the back of the wagon. His strength sapped, Quaid fell forward, landing prostrate. John Henry perceived a disturbance from behind. He turned and raised his double-barreled shotgun. He targeted a cowboy emerging from the pit in the wall. John Henry pulled the trigger, blasting the cowboy backwards. John Henry ran up to the riff to check on Samson. Looking into the abyss, he saw a bloodstained bear lying lifeless along with four cowboys. John Henry directed his voice outward. "Let's go! Get moving Sam!" he shouted.

Samantha struck the horses hard. The harnessed energy rolled the wagon down the alley. Reaching the intersection of the main street, Samantha turned the transport. A blast from beneath blew out the front wheels. It sent the whole team, wagon, and covered cargo, over onto it's side. The dust detonated as the wheeled barge broke. The eruption of earth buried the fallen. Gunfire broke out. John Henry came running forward, firing as he ran. Bullets crackled all around him. He quickly crouched behind a water barrel. To his left, he could see the toppled wagon. Samantha wiggled her way from behind the bodies of the overturned team. Stunned, Josephine attempted to stand. Dust dropped from the corners off her clothes. All was a daze. From across the street came a very unique sound. It was repetitive. It was the strafing of artillery. It was the firing of a Gatling gun. The bullets spread out over the street. In a pattern of destruction, they enshrouded John Henry. He dug in deep for added security. The sweep continued from left to right. The projectiles drew a line directly at Josephine. Perceiving the peril, she attempted to flee. Still in shock, Josephine was unaware of her footing. The hurried motion caused her to stumble. The rounds rang out loudly as they approached. The churning path of shells ignited the soil. Just as the explosions were to overcome her, Josephine felt a heavy weight land from above. The mass shielded her from the strikes. She felt the load tremble under the tremendous force of the impacts. A warm fluid drained down from the armored insulation. The liquid covered her clothes. It soaked through to her skin, bathing her in blood. The sound of the turret's rolling stopped. Josephine held her eyes closed tight. She pushed the form from atop her body. Rolling the figure over, Josephine saw the face of her father. It was Jacob Quaid. He had multiple permeations across his torso. The red ran out from his injuries. His breathing was slowed and labored. He lay motionless. Tears flowed over Josephine's cheeks. "Daddy, why?" she asked in distress.

Quaid glanced up. He smiled upon his Beloved. His matching green globes peered deep into his daughter's emerald eyes. "It is the greatest gift," he said softly. Josephine could not breathe seeing her fallen father. In a gasp Quaid whispered. "'Lord, now lettest thou servant depart in peace, according to thy word.'" (Luke 2:29) The spark of life in Quaid flickered. His gaze became fixed. His spirit left.

"No! Daddy, no!" Josephine shouted. Shots from atop the roof shattered the silence. There was no time to grieve. Josephine ran for the hardware store, leaving her father behind. John Henry and Samantha returned fire. Josephine took shelter behind the beams of the boardwalk. She drew her pistols. She pulled the trigger over and over in anger. The spray scattered across the wooden constructs on the opposite side of the street. With the loss of the Marshall, Samantha hardened her resolve. She released round after round of suppressive bombardment. As the Gatling gun was being reloaded, John Henry made for the wagon. Under duress, he grabbed several sticks of bundled dynamite. He thrust the TNT with all his strength in the direction of the weapon. Seeing her father's actions, Samantha took aim. As the airborne incendiary crossed the avenue, Sam squeezed off a killing shot. It triggered a large eruption near the gun's position. Josephine took off in a run. Driven by rage, she zigzagged through the street with extreme speed. Simultaneously, John Henry took up his hammer. With his great might, he swung the sledge into the support beam of the jailhouse's overhang. The ceiling crashed down upon three approaching assassins. The Gatling gun's operator cleared his vision. He readied the ammunition. While leaning down to reload, he heard a distinctive click. The cowboy glanced up. It was Josephine's colt. The gun barrel appeared as large as the sun. "Yield, or you shall surely perish," Josephine said sternly. After a single breath, metal rained down through the rooftop. The gunfire showered Josephine's position. She dove back against the store front wall, making herself as thin as air. The bullets split the rafters and killed the cowboy. The repetitive bursts blew holes in the framework, leaving a partially suspended aperture. Josephine drew in closer. A crushing bang exploded from the singularity of Samantha's rifle. This was followed by the thud of a lifeless form dropping to the street. It was over. Josephine raced back to her father's side. Quaid's color was pallid. Joey dropped to her knees. Placing her hands over her face, she wept.

It was morning. Josephine stood on the hill. It was the same hill on which her father had laid her mother to rest so many years before. Now, a second stone was erected as a monolithic tribute to a life left. Josephine hung her head, unable to watch the pallbearers lower her father's coffin into the ground. The mourners were many. The whole town turned out. Josephine, however, only felt isolation. She could not make out the minister's eulogy. The words seemed like so much unintelligible utterances. Josephine tried to take a deep breath. But the filling of her lungs with cool oxygen did not relax her state. She was inconsolable, and alone. The tears streamed down her face, detracting from her loveliness. But there is no beauty in death, she thought.

Weeks passed since Jacob Quaid was entombed. Josephine had not been seen. She buried herself inside her sorrow. Every day Samantha would make the trek from the Colonel's old place to the Marshall's front door. Pounding her fist firmly against the wood, she knocked. "Sister! Sister, it is me!" she shouted. No answer. Again came her exclamation. "Sister, please let me in!" No response. Each time the pattern reoccurred. Each day there was no motion, no reply. One Sunday morning, after the repetitive pleas went unnoticed, came a second knock. Josephine became frustrated with Samantha's persistence. She sat in silence at first. Another strike came, resounding. Josephine was infuriated by the sound. She got up from her chair. Through the dark she made her way to the rapping. Ready to tell Samantha off, Josephine flung open the door. Sam was not found at the entryway. It was Isa. He wore a tattered and tan smock, with sandals. He had a full beard. His hair was dark, long, and a little stringy. He smiled lovingly at Josephine.

"'Let mine eyes run down with tears night and day. And let them not cease. For the virgin daughter of my people is broken with a great break, with a very grievous blow,'" (Jer 14:17) he said to her.

Josephine began to cry. She hugged her friend and did not let go. Josephine felt his benevolent exterior girded by his inner strength. For the first time in weeks, she was happy to see someone standing on her porch. Josephine invited Isa inside. She opened the shutters, spilling light across the expanse of the room. Isa sat. Josephine followed. She placed herself next to him. She looked deep into his eyes. "Isa, why did it have to be?" asked Josephine. "Why Daddy?" she inquired sadly.

"'Except a corn of wheat fall into the ground and die, it abideth alone. But if it die, it bringeth forth much fruit,'" (John 12:24) Isa replied.

"I understand," said Josephine. "Yet, I feel so much anger. The hatred boils in my blood."

"'Be ye angry, and sin not,'" (Eph 4:26) said Isa.

Josephine was dismayed. In her despair, Josephine gave Isa a steely stare. She spoke to him in her contempt. "'But those mine enemies, which would not that I should reign over them, bring hither, and slay them before me.'" (Luke 19:27) she said.

Isa returned Josephine's outrage with calm. His eyes manifest a warming kindness. He smiled at her softly. "'If ye forgive not men their trespasses, neither will your Father forgive your trespasses,'" (Matt 6:14) Isa said gently. Josephine paused. Isa reached over and placed his hand on hers. "'Ye have heard that it was said by them of old time, thou shalt not kill. And whosoever shall kill, shall be in danger of the judgment,'" (Matt 5:21) he said.

Josephine's expression reverted to sorrow. Her grief was great. Such desolation was so unfamiliar. "What am I to do?" she asked.

Isa took up Josephine's hand in his and knelt to pray. Josephine followed his lead. Isa closed his eyes and began. "'Our Father which art in heaven, hallowed be thy name. Thy Kingdom come. Thy Will be done, in earth as it is in heaven. Give us this day our daily bread. And forgive us our debts, as we forgive our debtors. And lead us not into temptation, but deliver us from evil. For Thine is the kingdom, and the power, and the glory, forever.'" (Matt 6:9) Isa opened his eyes, turned his head, and smiled. Josephine felt a tender sensation flow through her spirit. It was tranquility. She sent an affectionate smile back. "'The Father, he shall give you another Helper. That he may abide with you forever,'" (John 14:6) he said. Isa stood. Josephine echoed his action. Isa continued. "'Peace I leave with you. My peace I give you. Not as the world giveth, give I unto you. Let not your heart be troubled, neither let it be afraid.'" (John 14:27) Josephine felt love.

"Please Isa," Josephine pleaded. "Do not go without me."

"'Whither I go, thou canst not follow me now. But thou shalt follow me afterwards,'" (John 13:36) he said.

"How will I know how to find you?" Josephine asked.

"'Whither I go ye know. And the way ye know,'" (John 14:4) he said. With that Isa turned and walked forth from her home. Josephine just watched as he faded in the distant sun.

10

The following Sunday morning it was Josephine who came knocking on Samantha's door. The sun had just risen above the horizon. It sprayed the foliage with particles of light. The dew glistened from the release of radiation. Sparkling reflections of promise lit the way to the dawn of a new day. Josephine rode with a renewed vigor. An appearance of peace glowed from behind her green eyes. With her contentment came confidence. Josephine's spirit was reborn. She smiled.

Josephine tied Bo to the porch of the old Colonel's place. She walked up the steps and rapped gently on the door. After a time, John Henry appeared. He looked down and smiled at Joey. He said nothing. His countenance told the story. In a restrained jubilance, John Henry turned and called out. "Samantha, someone is here to see you!"

"Who is it?" asked Sam loudly.

"Come and see," said John Henry. John Henry pulled back the door wider, revealing Josephine's face. In an Instant, Sam's irritation became joy. She ran out to greet her sister with an enormous hug. Sam tried to hold back her tears, but could not. Happiness overcame her.

"Josephine it is so good to see you here. I have missed you so," said Sam.

"And I you," said Joey. "I have come to ask for your company in the attendance church," she said to John Henry.

"Of course, my Lady," he replied. "We will be with you presently. So, please come in."

Upon reaching the chapel, the three dropped down from their rides. Samantha and John Henry headed up the stairs. Josephine stood fast. John Henry stopped and looked back. "My Lady, the time is short," he said. Josephine stared at John Henry and Samantha in apprehension. Samantha traveled back down the steps to her sister. She took Josephine's hand in hers. Without a word, Sam led Josephine into the church. Passing through the entranceway, all the parishioners turned to look at the Marshall's daughter. The assembly was hush. The clergyman broke the silence.

"Welcome back Miss Quaid," he said. Samantha, John Henry, and Josephine took their seats. The service started. Josephine listened but did not hear. She was lost in days past. Josephine's thoughts wandered back through time. She recalled sitting in the exact same spot every Sunday with her father by her side. As she drifted farther away, the sun changed position. The bright rays of light shone through the stained glass onto the now empty space. The fog lifted. Josephine opened her eyes to the spoken word.

"'Blessed be the God and Father of our Lord Jesus Christ, which according to his abundant mercy hath begotten us again unto a lively hope by the resurrection of Jesus Christ from the dead. To an inheritance incorruptible, and undefiled, and that fadeth not away, reserved in heaven for you,'" (1 Peter 1:3) said the minister.

The words warmed Josephine's heart. She was comforted by the memory of her father. Her spirit soared. Josephine engaged fully in the service. She happily took communion. Josephine shared handshakes, smiles, hugs, and pleasantries. She was home. Afterwards, Samantha addressed Josephine outside. "Hey, how about we have dinner out tonight?" Sam asked.

"Sounds good," replied Joey. "A day away from the stove will do me good."

"Great," said Sam. "I will meet you at the diner around five."

Josephine boarded the open wagon. Samantha climbed in next to her. With one stroke of the reins, the horses took to a trot. The ride home was quiet. Josephine felt calm after church. She did not want to disturb the calm by raising her voice over the roar of the wagon wheels. She would converse with Sam at dinner, she thought. The road was dry, hot, and dusty. The sky was a clear blue. Scattered white clouds floated across the stratosphere like leaves down a stream. There was a gentle breeze. It blew just enough to cool the skin. The trees seemed taller to Josephine. It was as if they had reached up to touch the ivory pillows drifting in the cerulean sea above. Looking at nature's beauty gave Josephine a strong reassurance that once again all was right in the world. She had the love of God. She had the love of her family. Her heart was full.

Later that day, Josephine rode Bo into town for supper. She hitched her ride and entered the diner. Samantha was waiting at a table near the center of the room. She smiled upon seeing her friend. Josephine sat. A waitress by the name Pearl came to greet them.

"Hello ladies," said Pearl.

"Good day," replied Josephine.

"We have some very good beef today. It was just delivered this morning," said Pearl.

"That sounds good," said Samantha.

"It comes with potatoes, all covered in a nice broth," said Pearl. "I know you ladies will like it. I had some earlier," she said.

"That is good enough for me," said Josephine. The server turned and headed for the kitchen, leaving the two sisters to talk. Sam started.

"Joey, father and I would like you to come and live with us. We are concerned about you staying in that house all by yourself," she said.

"I do not know," replied Joey.

"Please sister, come stay with us. We will make some new memories. Besides, we love you," said Sam.

"I will consider your offer. And I am aware that you and John Henry care about me. That, for now, is enough," said Joey.

"But we worry," said Sam.

"I would worry too!" shouted a voice from across the room.

The girl's heads turned in the direction of the exclamation. In the corner of the diner was a table with three cowboys. They were Mannix's men. Samantha stood up abruptly. She kicked her chair away, and withdrew her sidearm. "Shut up!" she screamed.

"Easy," replied the cowboy. "I am not addressing you," he said. "I am speaking to Miss Quaid." The cowboy stood slowly, then pointed a long bony finger at Josephine.

"So you know my name," replied Josephine. She stood sternly. "That means nothing to me," she said. "What is it they call you?"

"Ophis," he said. The cowboy smiled. His heinous grin was foul. Josephine could almost smell the noxious rotting of his teeth. A chill came through her. "Tell me girlie," he said. "After what happened to dear old dad, are you worried?"

"I fear no one," Josephine replied sternly. "Especially not the likes you."

"The likes of me?" Ophis laughed. "And what may that be, girlie?"

"You are a deceit," said Josephine. "You speak only lies."

"Lies!" cried Ophis. "Your father spoke of lies."

Josephine became visibly agitated. She moved around the table, taking a few steps in the direction of the cowboy. She kept her hands at her side, in a reserved posture. "You know not!" Josephine responded firmly.

"Your father claimed that your grandfather had an unmatched speed with the knife. He alleged that he could throw a blade faster than any man could draw his gun," said Ophis.

"That is true," said Josephine.

"Lies and more lies!" bellowed Ophis. Josephine's blood began to boil. "Your fabricator of a father said you possess that same skill. Another obvious lie," said Ophis.

"I do!" chided Josephine angrily.

"Well, well, well. Little girlie has claws," said Ophis.

Josephine stepped back, creating space. "I suggest you move along before there is trouble," she said.

"No trouble. No trouble at all, girlie," said Ophis.

"Time for you to go!" shouted Sam, staring down the cowboys.

Ophis started to move towards the door. He stopped, looking back at Josephine. "If you really fear no one, and if your father is no liar, prove it girlie," he said.

"I am also no fool," replied Josephine.

"No?" queried Ophis. "You are a child of lies, living a lie. If you can't prove your claim, then it is false."

The cowboy's words enraged Josephine. Her skin became flush. Her teeth clenched. Her hands closed tightly into fists. "If you are looking for a fight, you found one," said Josephine. "I will see you outside."

"With pleasure," responded Ophis.

"Stop this, Joey," said Sam. Josephine ignored her friend. She started to make her way past Sam towards the door. Samantha grabbed Josephine firmly by the arm. She pulled her in close. "'And Jesus answering said unto him. It is said thou shalt not tempt the Lord thy God,'" (Luke 4:12) Sam said with a whisper. She relinquished her grip and stepped back. Josephine looked deep into the austere eyes of brown which were her friend's.

"Okay, okay, we will leave," said Josephine.

Ophis saw Josephine's fury lapse. "Are you yellow, like your father?" he asked loudly. "He died a cowardice death, like a dog in the street." Josephine stopped. The words cut down to the quick. She bit her bottom lip in an attempt to control her anger.

Josephine grimaced through the pain. She glanced over to Sam, then slowly started to walk away. "Can't bear the truth, girlie?" questioned Ophis with a thunderous roar. "Oh yes, and I forgot," he said. "That pet of yours is also dead. Shame that his carcass is being eaten by the worms."

"Outside now deceiver!" Josephine screamed.

"My gun against your blade, girlie. We will see just who is the master of lies," said Ophis. He strode out of the diner. Josephine made for the door directly. She headed for the center of the street. Samantha ran after her friend.

"Joey this is a trap," said Sam. "This is what he wants. Think! Think hard. Do not fight him here, now. Walk away."

Josephine turned to her friend. "'Woe unto them that call evil good, and good evil. That put darkness for light, and light for darkness,'" (Ish 5:20) she said. "I am done running from the wicked."

Samantha realized that her sister was insistent. She saw the determination in her eyes. Samantha had seen that look before from the Marshall. Samantha relented. "Sister, if you must, you must," she said. "I will be watching."

"Thanks," said Josephine. She hesitated. "I will be careful," she said.

"There is no caution in a firefight," said Sam. "Make it quick."

Josephine looked up to see Ophis striding to the middle of the thruway. He stopped. "Girlie, I hope you are ready to die!" he shouted.

"I do not fear death," said Josephine.

"Then join your kin in the dirt," Ophis replied.

Josephine faced the cowboy. Her eyes followed his hands intently. Josephine slowly brushed back her top coat, revealing two belt knives in her waist. Ophis gave a grin. Samantha stood back and scanned the street. Her vision captured two cowboys concealed by the corner of the diner. She could see the barrels of the rifles targeting Josephine. This was no dual, it was a shooting gallery. The setup was meant to slay her sister. Samantha slowly slid from sight, passing behind the diner to flank the snipers. Josephine stared down her adversary. As she stood, motionless, her anger grew. She wanted the enemy to suffer. She wanted him dead. The covert cowboys waited with their sites trained on Josephine. As they concentrated on the shot, a small chuckle came from behind. "Drop 'em boys," said Sam. The cowboys were transfixed, seeing Samantha standing over them with both barrels drawn. "I know your boss would want a fair fight, right?" said Sam smiling.

Out in the street, the air was thick. Josephine's mouth was dry. A breeze blew through the concourse. Both warriors waited, and watched. Josephine held fast. She could see Ophis begin to perspire. His eye twitched. Then it came. His thumb moved. Josephine threw. Both blades crossed the expanse, impaling her tormentor. One dug deep into Ophis' right shoulder. The cowboy had trouble pulling the trigger. The other struck his left thigh. He dropped down to the earth in agony. Josephine coolly approached the killer. Standing above him, she glared at the demon with disdain.

"Go ahead," said Ophis. "I know you want to."

Josephine knelt close. She grasped the projectile protruding from his leg. An intense rage overwhelmed her. "'Eye for eye, tooth for tooth, hand for hand, foot for foot. Burning for burning, wound for wound, and stripe for stripe!'" (Ex 21:24) Josephine twisted the handle. Ophis cried in excruciating agony.

"Grievous delight, girlie! I can see your Black heart. Finish it now!"

Bang! Bang! Bang! From behind Josephine came gunfire. The vibrations pierced the sky. Josephine turned and saw John Henry holding his gun straight into the air. He stared at her with indignation. "It is over Josephine," he yelled.

"It is never over," shouted Josephine. "Evil is pervasive!"

"Killing him will not change that!" John Henry replied loudly. "It will change you though."

"No! Not after what they did to father," Josephine screamed.

"Do not to do this," John Henry implored.

"What then?" Josephine queried spitefully.

"I believe you know the answer," said John Henry while slowly approaching her station. He holstered his weapon and continued to move steadily toward Josephine. John Henry reached behind his back, and pulled out a pair of handcuffs. "Go bind Sam's captives. Then bring them to the jailhouse," he said. John Henry held out the shackles as Josephine glared back at him. "Do as I say. You are no murderer, Josephine," he said.

"You do not know me," she said in anger.

"Yes, yes I do," said John Henry. "You are the daughter of Jacob Quaid, a man who gave his life for you. Make that life mean something." Josephine looked down at Ophis. John Henry turned to her. "'A righteous man falling down before the wicked is as a troubled fountain, and a corrupt spring,'" (Prov 25:26) he said. Josephine took the cuffs from him. She made her way over to Sam. She spoke no further.

11

Daybreak. New beginnings bring new hope. On this day all hope was lost. The sun rose but it did not shine. Clouds clast shades of grey through the sky. A sadness hung in the air like the knell of a bell. Josephine stared out the window, a spectre of herself. Her father, her mentor and protector, had passed. Her champion, her comrade and companion, was gone. Her friendships, her strength and support, were strained. Her faith, her sanctum and security, had faded. All of her world was wiped away. She stood in absence. Josephine could not stomach the sorrow. The melancholy made her sick. The pain welled up inside, driving a blackened bile into her throat. Tears fell from the pools of green and blue. The droplets ran down her face without regard. Hopelessness. Helplessness. Heartache. Her spirit crushed, she knew not what to do. After a time, Josephine knelt and prayed. "'And He said unto me, son of man, can these bones live? And I answered. O Lord God, thou knowest. Again he said to me, prophesy upon these bones, and say unto them, O ye dry bones, hear the word of the Lord. This saith the Lord

God unto these bones. Behold, I will cause breath to enter into you, and ye shall live.'" (Eze 37:3) Josephine remained on her knees, her hands clasped, her head bent. Time passed. Still, her angst persisted. She cried out in pain. "Lord, all that was the best of me is no more. Why must I suffer so? Why do you not to help me?" The answer came in the form of a knock. Someone was tapping, gently, on Josephine's door. She opened the egress. There, stood Samantha.

"Good morning," said Samantha.

"What is good about it?" questioned Josephine snidely.

Samantha simply smiled back at her. "It is good to see you too sister," she said. Josephine remained unmoved. "Aren't you going to invite me in?" asked Sam.

Josephine stirred from her trance. "Yes, sorry Sam," she said. "Come in." Samantha stepped through the entranceway. She strolled into the front room and sat. "Can I get you anything?" asked Josephine.

"Yes, my sister back," said Sam with some sarcasm.

Josephine gave a stern look. "I am who I am," she replied.

"No, you are not," insisted Samantha. She approached Josephine. "You keep your self hidden. You reject father and me. And you often speak in anger," she said. Samantha paced. Through her agitation, she continued. "Now you act like the madman you once abhorred." Samantha calmly reached out to touch her friend. "You are the Marshall's daughter," she said with love. "And you are God's child." She paused. "Remember?" Josephine became changed. She slowly stepped back and sat. She was embarrassed by the scolding. Samantha rested next to her friend. She looked deep into Josephine's green eyes. Samantha saw the anguish that lay behind them. Sam continued. "'Bearth all things, believeth all things, hopeth all things, endureth all things.'" (1 Cor 13:7) Josephine smiled at her sister. "The only question is, what will you do now?" inquired Sam.

"I am unsure," replied Josephine. She glanced idly around the room. "I am in trouble, Sam," she said.

"We will help," replied Sam. Samantha's words stirred up a memory inside Josephine. It was of a story she had heard from her father long ago. He had told her that if she ever found herself in despair, to go into the wilderness and light three fires. Then, he said, the Helper will come.

"The Helper," whispered Josephine under her breath.

"What?" asked Sam.

"I must go," said Joey.

"Why would you run away?" asked Sam.

"Not away," said Joey. "Toward."

"Toward what?" questioned Sam.

"I will go forward and find the Helper," replied Josephine.

"Who is that?" asked Sam.

"I do not know," said Joey. "I only know that my father said to seek him if I ever came to this place in time."

"That does not make sense," said Sam.

"I have faith in my father's words," said Joey. "Therefore, I must try."

"Okay, okay," said Sam with a grin. "Just come back safe to us. We love you."

"I will my sister, I will," said Joey. She smiled back at Sam in full expression.

That night Josephine was restless. She tossed and turned, sleepless. Her slumber did not come easy. What did come was a vivid dream. As Josephine's fatigue finally overcame her anxiety, she faded. While she slept, Josephine perceived a strong presence. She rolled over to see the face of her father sitting on the edge of the bed. It seemed real. Josephine looked into his emerald eyes. Jacob Quaid smiled back lovingly. "What troubles you, my Beloved?" asked Quaid. Josephine sat up, still stunned. Bewildered by the ghost, she did not speak at first. The amazing elation in viewing her father's visage was overwhelming. She ultimately addressed him.

"I feel lost," she said softly.

"How so?" asked Quaid.

"I have no direction without you," Josephine replied.

"Remember what I taught you. Always know that I am here, Beloved," said Quaid holding his hand to his heart.

"I miss you, Daddy," said Josephine starting to cry. Quaid smiled in reassurance. He slowly reached to comfort his daughter. Abruptly, Quaid's countenance changed. His appearance became ashen. His eyes widened. He moved his mouth, yet no words came forth. Josephene's euphoria morphed into apprehension. Fear spread across Quaid's face. A large black python slithered across the floor. It wrapped itself around Quaid's legs and trunk. The serpent was dark, with a silvery shine to it's scales. The pattern was hypnotic. His eyes were of orange, as a newly washed pumpkin. His forked tongue flickered in and out of it's glottis, giving Josephine a chill. The constrictor quickly engulfed Quaid's form. The coils contracted with an immense power. The crushing of the Quaid's circulation led to ischemia. Quaid struggled to remain conscious. Weakened, he rolled backward, falling from the bed. Josephine reached to clasp his hand but could not. Quaid hit the floor hard. The giant increased it's grip. Quaid cringed as it's hold became tighter and tighter. Josephine tried to scream but could not. The reptile wound upward encircling Quaid's neck. Quaid turned his head, fighting the pain. He looked directly at his daughter in desperation.

"Do not let me be taken," he said.

Josephine watched in horror as the snake opened his mouth to swallow her father. She drew a deep breath. In distress she cried out, "No!" Josephine awoke in a sweat. There was a bitter taste in her mouth. Her heart raced. She looked around. She saw nothing. Her father's macabre extermination flashed through her mind. Josephine became ill. After the purge came anger. No longer distraught by the night terror, Josephine became resolute. She washed up. She cleansed herself of the emesis and of the nightmare. She moved forward.

Josephine packed several days rations. They consisted of dried fruit, salted pork, and coffee beans. She drew as much water from the well as she thought Bo could carry. Lastly, she strolled out to the barn and saddled her horse. With a hitch and a kick, off Bo went. Where, Josephine knew not. It was a leap of faith. For three days Josephine rode into the wilderness. Near the end of the third day, she came across an unusual plain. It was protected by a mountain ridge on a single side. Each of the surrounding terrains were unique. One was of grass. One consisted of tall trees. The last was of stone. Josephine stopped and dismounted by the rising rock formation. The sun glistened on the surfaces creating a hardened and cold complexion. The color was a steel blue, almost as ice. Josephine felt comfort here. She made camp. Josephine collected branches of wood to construct the trinity fires. She made three large piles, then set them ablaze. Afterwards, she settled Bo for the night. Josephine then sat and ate. Tired from the journey, Josephine rolled out her bedding and fell fast asleep.

Josephine broke her repose in full daylight. Wiping the night's rest from her eyes, she saw a large surrounding hoard of men. Josephine slowly stood to address the band of natives occupying her camp. She did not feel fear, but she was aware that caution should be taken. Josephine smiled. The tension did not ease. She stepped forward. "Do you speak any English?" she asked. No reply. "I travel in peace," she said. No native spoke. "Okay then," she said. "I understand. This is your land. I will move along." The tribesmen approached her position. Josephine remained calm as they closed in. She did not draw her weapon. The men grabbed her firmly. One bound her hands as another wrapped a kerchief around her eyes. In the darkness, she was lifted up onto the back of Bo. Once on horseback, Josephine rode blind in the day's shiny hot sun. Upon arrival to their destination, she was let down gently. Josephine remained like a tombstone as a clattering commotion encircled her. She could hear loud voices echo about. Through the turmoil, Josephine felt footsteps. With a great deal of surprise, the sound of perfect English resounded out.

"Why do you bring me this girl?" a voice asked in agitation. With a firm pull, Josephine's blindfold was ripped away. In front of her was an old native with black braided hair. One tail laid to each side. His face was weathered, wrinkled, and scarred. Josephine peered deep into his aging eyes. The tribesman stood still as a star. After a time, in a whisper he uttered, "Green Eyes..." Josephine stared as a small saline drop formed under his eyelid. The old warrior advanced forward. He reached out for her. He placed his arms around Josephine, and drew her close. He held her tight against his chest. Pulling back, he longingly looked into Josephine's eyes of silver and green. The verdant crystalline orbs sparkled in the sunlight. In a burst of excitement, the old warrior exclaimed in his native language, "My brother has come back!" A roar broke throughout the entire tribe. Each warrior howled as if celebrating a great victory. The shrieks filled the air and reverberated across the plains to the heavens. The old warrior addressed Josephine in English. "You have my brother's eyes."

"Your brother?" asked Josephine.

"Yes, you are a Quaid are you not?" said the warrior. Josephine paused. "I called him Green Eyes," continued the warrior. "I am Red Cloud, the leader of this tribe. Welcome."

Josephine's mind stuttered in an attempt to put the pieces together. Finally, the complete comprehension came. "You are the Red Prince," she said in understanding.

"Yes," he replied. My brother said he would return to me on the day of the trinity fire. I have since waited for that time. And now, he has come back to me, in you. My heart sings with great joy today." Red Cloud took Josephine's hand in his. He smiled gently. "Come," he said. "Let us talk in the comfort of my home." Josephine clasped the chief's hand tight. She followed him to his tent. Josephine dipped her head to enter the tall triangular structure. Outside, the coarse canvas seemed small. Inside, the tepee was multifaceted. It had a multitude of color. Luxurious blankets and beads filled the space. Woven baskets sat around the perimeter. The scene was a kaleidoscope of comfort. Red Cloud sat. He motioned for Josephine to follow. She acknowledged the invitation, and placed herself slowly on the ground. "I have much to tell," he said. "You see, I loved your grandfather, and he loved me. We brothers met when I was very young. He came into my life by saving it." Somewhat confounded by his statement, Josephine looked upon the old warrior with confusion. He continued. "I was on a morning hunt. I had gone deep into the woods, far from my home. Hours of tracking game led me to the base of the large rock. I sat in the shade to rest. My fatigue overcame me. I fell asleep. In the middle of my slumber, a strong sound startled me. I awoke to find a grizzly, bearing down on me. I had no time to react. In seconds the beast was on top of me. I struggled for my life. His enormous weight crushed my chest, breaking several ribs. I labored to breathe. I could not even move enough air to scream. His fangs bit through my skin around my face and neck. I felt the flow of warm blood trickle from the incisions of his incisors. Claws ripped across my abdomen, like the gutting of a fish. I saw death. As I lost consciousness, there came a great jerk. The bear drew back. Through the red haze, I saw your grandfather's face as he killed the beast." The old warrior paused to gather himself. His emotion ran high. He turned his gaze away from Josephine for a moment. He took a deep breath. Back in control, he continued. "Your grandfather could have left me to die. He did not. He carried me for miles back to my camp. There, he was greeted by suspicion and cruelty. Unfortunately, as I lay unresponsive, he endured torture and pain. Days passed before I could speak, and finally intervene. I owed him my life, and he was met with contempt and brutality. I was ashamed. Through all that he endured, your grandfather still found it in his heart to forgive. That gesture I have never forgotten. And I never will. From then on we were brothers." The old warrior looked lovingly at Josephine. He smiled. "We two grew, as we grew up together. I taught him the bow, how to hunt, and to ride. I instructed him in the ways of my people. In turn, he schooled me in English. But more importantly, he showed me the great love of God. I learned of His everlasting love and of the Son who gave himself for our eternal life. For all he had given me, I pledged my endless devotion. You see my Beloved, my brother had loved me before he ever knew me." The old warrior placed his hands over Josephine's, holding them tight. "'We love Him, because He first loved us,'" (1 John 4:19) said Red Cloud with introspection. "This knowledge changes a man, even an old warrior such as I. So, welcome... And much love, my child."

Josephine smiled a broad smile. "I am pleased to meet you, uncle," she said. "And I am honored to be invited into your camp."

"Might I ask, how is my godson?" inquired Red Cloud. Josephine hung her head, unable to speak. "What is it?" asked Red Cloud.

"He was killed," replied Josephine softly.

"I see," said Red Cloud sadly.

The volume of Josephine's voice slightly increased. "My father's memory led me here. I have come seeking help."

"I will do all I can," replied Red Cloud.

"Thank you," said Josephine. "But I will need many to defeat this foe."

"We, your family, are," said Red Cloud. "'We being many, are one body in Christ, and every one members, one of another,'" (Romans 12:5) he said. Josephine expressed happiness. She felt the affection emanating from the old warrior. "The sun, the moon, and the sky may pass away, but my love will never fade," he said. Red Cloud rose and walked out from his dwelling. He made for the middle of camp. There, he lifted his arms upward. All stopped their activities. "I have been asked to combat a great evil. Over the years, I have encouraged a life of peace. This day, however, my brother has sent me a message of immense concern. There is a growing corruption in a nearby land. This destructive force threatens our family. I aim to take up arms against this wickedness. I stand here now to ask the aid of all good men to help me defeat this enemy." Red Cloud bent down onto his right knee and looked up.

"'According to the eternal purpose which He purposed in Christ Jesus our Lord. In whom we have boldness and access with confidence by the faith of him. Wherefore I desire that ye faint not at my tribulations for you, which is your glory. For this cause I bow my knees unto the Father our Lord Jesus Christ, of whom the whole family in heaven and earth is named.'" (Eph 3:11) With that, Red Cloud stood and faced his brethren. "Warriors arise!" he shouted. "And fight!" A great cry coursed throughout the land, as each warrior joined their voice to his.

12

It was night. The darkness shone down it's brilliance upon the lone western town. Miles outside the city limits, there was a ranch. Mannix was held up within the structure. Deep in the bowels he toiled. In a solitary room, a single lamp gave light. The illuminating flicker of the flame cast shadows across the walls like demons dancing. The gloaming gave off a chill. It was a bitter cold, as if being wrapped in ice. Inside this pouch, he sat. Mannix poured over the accounts he had cast out onto his desk. The large wooden framed desk from which he worked was of a deep color. It was almost as if the timber had been burned by fire. The legs were thick at the top, turning down the calves to the hooves. It's wood was engraved in circular rows like Capricorn. The tabletop was flat with jagged ends, which were sharp like teeth. His chair was grand. It had a tall back with a padded support. The chair was amber, a deep blood red. The burgundy handrests had the faces of growling dogs. The support consisted of two pointed spires. And in betwixt them was the crest of a great dragon.

A knock at the door drew Mannix from his thoughts. "Come in," he said. The door opened and Ophis stepped into the pitch.

"Sorry to disturb, sir," he said. "But there is an issue."

Mannix directed his attention upward. "What is it?" he asked.

"The girl is back," said Ophis.

"What girl?" asked Mannix.

"The Marshall's daughter," replied Ophis.

"She is of no consequence to me," retorted Mannix. "Just a footnote in our conquest."

"Very well, sir," said Ophis. The lieutenant turned and left the room quietly. Mannix returned to his papers, self-possessed.

Josephine was back at home. She had kept appearances low. She limited her time outdoors. She ventured outside only to travel to the barn, where she tended to Bo. Days following her return, Josephine was startled to find Samantha sitting in the front room, silently. "So, were you ever going to tell me that you were back?" asked Sam.

"Why have you come?" asked Joey.

"I wanted to see my friend. And to ask if there was anything you required," said Sam.

"I am, happy to see you too, Sam," said Joey. "And now that you have asked, I could use a favor."

"What might that be?" asked Sam.

"The outlaw, Mannix, I plan to jail him," said Joey. "Are you in?"

"It has been tried before," replied Sam.

"Are you in or out then?" asked Joey sternly.

"You can count on me, sissy," said Sam.

"How do you think John Henry will feel about this?" asked Joey.

"He is his own man," said Sam. "He has steered clear of Mannix. His men number near one hundred. Father is only one man."

"What if he had help?" asked Joey.

"He sent word to the United States Army months ago," said Sam. "He has heard no reply."

"Tell him I can guarantee an arrest," replied Joey. Sam looked directly at her friend. She saw the conviction of an inspired consciousness. Josephine gave a reassuring smile. She placed one hand gently on to Sam's shoulder. "Trust me," she said.

"I do," said Sam. "With my life."

Sam left the Marshall's place and headed for home. Upon returning, she found John Henry waiting. "Where have you been?" asked John Henry.

"Josephine has returned," said Samantha. "So, I went for a visit."

"I see," said John Henry.

"Father," said Samantha. "I need to talk to you about an important matter."

"Okay, what might that be?" asked John Henry.

"Josephine has asked me for my assistance," said Samantha.

"And how can I help?" asked John Henry.

"Josephine is determined to put a stop to Mannix," replied Samantha.

"You two are going to get yourselves killed," said John Henry with intensity. "Remember what happened to the

Marshall?" Samantha was silent. "We must wait for the army to arrive," said John Henry. "We need more manpower."

"Wake up, father!" exclaimed Samantha. "They are not coming. This is our fight. We must confront this evil!"

"I admire your courage, my daughter. But reality tells a different tale," said John Henry. "All lives will be lost."

Samantha stared straight into her father's eyes. "'And he that taketh not his cross, and followeth after me, Is not worthy of me. He that findeth his life shall lose it. And he that loseth his life for my sake shall find it,'" (Matt 10:38) said Samantha. She looked lovingly at her father. "This, we must do."

John Henry turned his back on his daughter. After a time, he circled back around. "Yes, my love, you are right," he said. "This, we must do."

Morning broke over the night's watch at the Mannix ranch. The twenty men patrolling the perimeter had come together at the fortified ridge centered fifty yards in front of the old farmhouse. The fighting hole was an elongated trench lined by earth-filled gabions. The woven barrier provided protection from the surface to about four feet above. The men could move parallel to the blockade without exposure. It's presence made the farmhouse seem more like a fortress. The cowboys were all smiles at the prospect of a warm meal, and an even warmer bed. The lively chatter broke into laughter. As Ophis approached with a group of fresh replacements, the sun began to rise. The horizon became bathed in a glittering gold. The pink ball of flame grew from a semicircle into a lavender globe. The star's rays of rouge colored patterns of purple into a bluing sky. One of the cowboys looked into the celestial light, and saw a single shadow atop a horse. "What is that?" he asked, pointing at the figure. The cowboys turned their heads in unison. They regarded the sole rider. The twenty stood stunned. Ophis stepped out from the crowd to get a better look. He slowly walked up the incline, allowing the rider to see him in full view. After walking several yards, Ophis heard a voice cry across the wind.

"Ophis! You, your boys, and your boss, are all under arrest!" the voice shouted.

After a time, Ophis recognized the verbal vexation. He smiled in disbelief. "Little girl, you talk big!" he shouted. "But talk is not action!" Ophis raised his arms out to his side. "If you want me, come and get me!"

"This is your last chance to surrender," screamed Josephine. "Or shall I come down there and take you by force?"

Ophis faced the cowboys and laughed. He spun back around toward Josephine wearing a wicked grin. "All by yourself, little girlie?" he asked in ridicule.

"No!" replied Josephine. "I have brought friends!" With that assertion, three riders appeared on the crest of the peak. Samantha, John Henry, and Red Cloud, rode up alongside Josephine. Ophis placed his fingers in his mouth and gave a loud whistle. Another twenty cowboys came running from the barracks house, fully loaded.

"Four against forty!" yelled Ophis. "I'll take that bet!"

Josephine raised a war spear over her head. It was a brown wooden spike of alternating red and white bands. It was approximately seven feet in length. It had feathers that flew at spaced intervals, which blew gently in the breeze. Josephine held it horizontal to the plain. All time stopped. Josephine stared deep into the abyss. The field before her seemed to elongate. It began to revolve. Round and around it spun, stretching, then becoming black. Beneath her breath Josephine whispered. "This Shakespeare is for you Daddy... 'Once more unto the breach, dear friends, once more.'" Josephine dropped her hand. Upon the lowering of the spear, one hundred warriors rode over the ridge. They formed a line extending across the entire hilltop. The queue stood as a great wall of goodness. The linear formation of nobility displayed the faces of painted men on horseback. Most had stripes of red or white descending from the zygomatic process, going to the inferior mandible. Others had color that originated in the corners of the orbicularis oris, then crossed the master muscle. Many had black bands of pigment like masks over the eyes. Feathers of different colors and numbers adorned their long hair. Every warrior carried a weapon. Each had a bow, a spear, or a war club. The war club was constructed of a carved rock banded to a reed handle. The shaft was long like a polo mallet. Several warriors had Henry rifles at their side. All were ready to engage the enemy. It became quiet. Josephine held her spear tight. In a swift single motion she raised the weapon and shouted, "Go!"

The lit fuse set off an explosion of hooves. The rampaging riders ramrodded down the ridge. The beasts kicked up dust and debris, creating a wake of spewed soil. The warriors gave out a howl that pierced the air. The battle had begun. The ranch hands rifles discharged, releasing a fury of projectiles. The barrage of bullets cut through the atmosphere like bolts of lightning. Many struck their targets, knocking holes into the wave of attackers. Josephine pushed Bo forcefully forward, dodging the darts. She fired her handguns repeatedly as she rode. Samantha and John Henry dove into the fray, blasting balls of lead as they went. Red Cloud, the ultimate refinement in horsemen, blew by with both hands clasping his bow. With extreme speed, the arrows soared from his string. They struck, time after time, impaling the adversary. As the fighting force made their way down the hillside, lines of rope were raised from the earth, eclipsing the riders. Once downed, the warriors took heavy casualties. An old nemesis fired from the fortification. The large metal machine took aim. The revolving rifled grooves spun in the cylinder of the Gatling gun. The cranked carousel contained cartridges of ammunition, which loaded each bullet into the back. The firing pins ejected round after round of suppressing fire. The raining balls fell like hail. It poured. The advancing warriors were cut down like falling trees. Josephine and Samantha leapt from their horses and crawled for cover. Out of immediate danger, the two continued to return fire. John Henry was hit. He laid back as the battle raged on, with both sides feeding the flames of the fight.

"We have to take out that gun!" shouted Sam.

"We are pinned down," replied Joey.

"I have an idea," said Sam.

"Okay, I am listening," said Joey.

"I will smash into the center, exposing the gunner. Then you take him out with your Whitworth," said Sam.

"Absolutely not!" screamed Joey. "It is a fool's errand!"

"We need to take the advantage," shouted Sam. "This is the only way!"

"No! I will not allow it. We will find another path!" exclaimed Joey. Once having said the words, another volley came crashing around them. The eruptions blew up the surrounding soil. Josephine ducked down, closing her eyes. A loud whistle broke through the surge. Josephine spun around to see Sam leaping onto Kush. Josephine jumped up in an attempt to stop her. "No!" she screamed. With a single kick, Sam was off. She stayed low, and lateral to the ground. Tucked in tight to her steed, Sam held on for her life. She thought of what the Marshall had once told her, that force equals mass times velocity. Sam sped up, increasing the oncoming force. She urged the animal faster and faster, and created a collision course. She drove Kush down the field and directly into the wall of gabions. Joey readied the long rifle. She took aim. Sam went airborne as the horse slammed through the barrier. Seeing the exposed gunner, Joey pulled the trigger. The gunner was struck as a hammer hits a pin, blowing him backwards.

Red Cloud reared up, rallying the warriors to attack. Red Cloud ran wild. He rapidly released arrow after arrow. Repeatedly, the flying spikes impaled their quarry. Driving through the gap in the gabions, he clipped the cowboys with his war club, dealing death blows. Such ferocity Josephine had never seen. The cowboy's blood spilled across his body, escalating the madness. Josephine called for Bo. He galloped to her position. Josephine mounted, and took off in full stride. She zigzagged through the flying debris. Josephine needed to find her friend. Josephine fired her pistols as she rode. She pressed the bombardment hard with both barrels. Josephine dropped man after man as she made her way to Samantha. The warriors continue the attack. The cowboys scattered and ran. The route was on.

Josephine reached the abandoned wall. She drove Bo through the gap. On the other side she saw Samantha lying lifeless. Josephine leapt down and rushed to her side. Josephine removed her hat. She used it to support her sister's head. "Sam, can you speak?" she asked. Samantha's eyes rolled back like that of a doll. Josephine's heart stopped. She gasped. Josephine drew closer to her friend. She leaned over and whispered. "'For I will restore health unto thee, and I will heal thee of thy wounds, saith the Lord.'" (Jer 30:17) Samantha's lips moved. Her chest rose. Josephine's hope came to life. Joey smiled at her sister. "Anything broken?" she asked.

"I do not think so," said Sam.

"Can you walk?" asked Joey.

"I will try," replied Sam.

"Good," said Joey. "Get yourself to John Henry. I will press on."

Josephine grabbed the Gatling gun. She targeted the remaining ranch hands and held fast. The victory, led by Red Cloud and his warriors was just about complete. Those who were not captured were in full retreat. To the left of Josephine's feet lay Ophis. He was inanimate. She swung the gun high into the air. In a moment of instability, Josephine cranked the machine in a state of psychosis. She let out a great cry. The pandemonium stopped. The enemy dropped their weapons. Red Cloud signaled his warriors to cease hostilities. No need of more killing, thought Josephine. The Marshall's daughter looked to her uncle. "I am going after Mannix," she said.

"I will not stop you," replied Red Cloud.

Josephine made her way to the front door of the main house. The large double doors were thick and wooden. A metal handle adorned each entry. Above the portal was a stone sign. The slab was cobbled with Aramaic writing. Josephine went in. The layout was circular. She glanced right, then left. She saw no one. Josephine moved toward the center of the spiraled sphere. At the core of the house was a door. Josephine opened it. She saw Mannix sitting calmly behind a desk. The sawtoothed tabletop was covered with papers and maps. Mannix sat up in his high backed chair. "Come in," he said.

"I do not need an invitation," said Josephine holding her pistol on him. "You are under arrest." Josephine moved slowly into the room. Mannix gave a grin as she approached.

"What do you hope to gain by this?" asked Mannix.

"Justice," said Josephine.

"Justice is for fools," said Mannix. "This world is not just. And it never will be. This is a fallen world, and the fallen shall rule it."

"You shall not! You will be imprisoned. You, will not get to see what happens to this world," replied Josephine.

"Kill me then," he said. "You know you want to."

"No," said Josephine. "I will do what is right."

"Right does not always win," said Mannix with a sneer.

"It does today," retorted Josephine. She approached his position. As Josephine came within a few feet, he slid his chair slightly back from the desk as if to surrender. Mannix put his hands to his side. He glanced over at an open drawer hiding a handgun. A sharp singing sound split the air. An arrow pierced

Mannix's right arm. Josephine peered around the impaled menace to see a small Derringer in the desk drawer. Looking back, she saw Red Cloud standing at the entrance, bow in hand.

"I would not move," said Red Cloud. "Maybe she will not, but I will."

"A Derringer, how dramatic," said Josephine as she took Mannix captive.

Years passed. The one western town grew older, as did Josephine. She went from young lady to young woman. Time found her in the bedroom of the Marshall's home. Around her was found her friends, John Henry, Red Cloud, and Samantha. She held a brand-new baby boy. Samantha sat on the edge of the bed looking at her sister with great joy. John Henry and Red Cloud stood at her side. Josephine was a mother. She held the newborn tight. Lovingly, she smiled at him.

"What will be his name?" asked Samantha.

"'The thing that hath been, it is that which shall be. And that which is done is that which shall be done,'" (Ecc 1:9) said Josephine. She smiled at her family. "So, I will call him Isa."